REBECCA WINTERS

The Royal
Marriage Arrangement

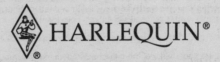

TORONTO • NEW YORK • LONDON
AMSTERDAM • PARIS • SYDNEY • HAMBURG
STOCKHOLM • ATHENS • TOKYO • MILAN • MADRID
PRAGUE • WARSAW • BUDAPEST • AUCKLAND

Recycling programs
for this product may
not exist in your area.

ISBN-13: 978-0-373-17567-3
ISBN-10:   0-373-17567-1

THE ROYAL MARRIAGE ARRANGEMENT

First North American Publication 2009.

Copyright © 2008 by Rebecca Winters.

www.eHarlequin.com

Printed in U.S.A.

Rebecca Winters, whose family of four children has now swelled to include five beautiful grandchildren, lives in Salt Lake City, Utah, in the land of the Rocky Mountains. With canyons and high Alpine meadows full of wildflowers, she never runs out of places to explore. They, plus her favorite vacation spots in Europe, often end up as backgrounds for her Harlequin Romance® novels, because writing is her passion, along with her family and church. Rebecca loves to hear from her readers. If you wish to e-mail her, please visit her Web site at www.cleanromances.com.

This month Prince Lucca makes Alexandra his convenient bride, but only Lucca's love can make her feel truly royal.

The Royal Marriage Arrangement

Next month, Rebecca Winters brings you another regal romance from THE ROYAL HOUSE OF SAVOY as Crown Princess Regina hopes her gardener will become her groom!

Italian Groom, Princess Bride

Share your dream wedding proposal
and you could win a stunning diamond necklace!

For more information
visit www.DiamondBridesProposal.com.

CHAPTER ONE

"How much is still owing to satisfy the creditors, Mr. Watkins?"

The aging attorney raised his shaggy gray eyebrows. "Twelve million dollars."

Alex's heart plunged to her feet. That much? She felt the worst about Manny Horowitz. Her mother's agent was a good man who'd done everything to further her mother's career all these years. He was still owed close to two million dollars. How could her mother not have paid him?

"I've auctioned everything except my mother's diamonds. They've got to cover it!"

Jewelry was the only thing remaining for Alex to sell from her mother's Beverly Hills estate. If she couldn't meet the sum, then the tabloids would hear of it and trash her mother's blighted reputation even more than they'd already done by exploiting her drug-related death. Some whispered that after her last divorce from Sheik Mustafah Tahar, Kathryn Carlisle had committed suicide, but nothing had been proved conclusively. Alex didn't know what to believe.

"I'm sorry it's come to this, Alexandra. A child shouldn't have to be burdened this way."

"Thank you, Mr. Watkins, but I haven't been a child for

a long time." In fact, she'd been through so much already as the unwanted offspring of the world's most beautiful woman that Alex felt ancient, but she supposed twenty-five still sounded young to him.

Since her mother's death on Christmas morning five months ago, Mr. Watkins had bent over backward to help her find ways to pay off her mother's debts. Furthermore he'd never once said a bad thing about her narcissistic parent who'd been married and divorced six times. As Kathryn's attorney from the beginning of her career, he'd had more right than anyone to castigate the willful, infamous Hollywood phenomenon of the film world who'd disregarded his advice and had run through money like she did alcohol.

At only forty-five years of age Kathryn Carlisle had come to a shockingly ugly end with nothing to show for it but a history of disastrous marriages, explosive divorces, unpaid bills despite her millions and a criminally neglected child from her first failed union. "Where would you suggest I go to get the best price for her jewelry?"

"The House of Savoy on Fifth Avenue in New York."

"My father gave her a diamond bracelet from there on their wedding night."

It was the only thing Alex remembered her mother telling her about her father. As Alex had matured she had learned for herself that her father, Oleg Grigory, had owned one of the biggest casinos in Las Vegas. When she'd grown old enough to understand, she'd heard rumors that he had ties to the Russian mafia, but no one knew for sure. His early death in an airplane crash was purported to be the work of a rivaling mob family.

Mr. Watkins nodded. "Without question they're the world's expert on diamonds."

Alex frowned because it meant paying for an airline ticket to the East Coast. She would have to juggle her bills to come up with the money, but Alex's mother had claimed she possessed a king's ransom in diamonds from her various husbands. If that were true, maybe all her debts would be satisfied. Only then could Alex bury the past and try to get on with her life.

"I'll call you as soon as I've booked my flight."

"Good. Considering we're talking about your mother's collection, I feel they're the one company that will be totally honest in their dealings with you. And…discreet."

Ah, yes. Discreet. For this last, financial transaction, maybe it would be best to get away from Hollywood and the scandalmongers.

Oh, Mother… Why couldn't you have been a mother *instead of Kathryn Carlisle?*

Mr. Watkins eyed her with compassion. "Once you know your flight, I'll make the appointment for you with the head jeweler. Drop by the bank on your way to the airport, and I'll arrange for them to hand over the jewel case from her strongbox."

With a nod she left his office and headed for her job as a makeup artist on a studio lot. She would have to talk to her boss, Michelle, about getting some time off. The older woman who headed the department had always been good to her and would certainly let Alex take the time she needed, but this was the last favor she intended to ask of her.

A few days later Alex stepped out of a New York taxi into unseasonable June heat and humidity. She checked her watch. It was 10:20 a.m. That gave her ten more minutes.

Alex imagined the temperature would soar by the afternoon and congratulated Mr. Watkins for getting her an early appointment at the House of Savoy.

After gripping her purse and the small overnight bag carrying the jewel case and one change of clothes, she started across the intersection toward the exclusive store. To her surprise there was a long line of people that went from its entrance and down the street to disappear around the next corner. Security was everywhere. She approached one of the women standing there reading a book.

"Excuse me?" The other woman looked up, not particularly happy to be bothered. "What's going on here? Why is there such a long line?"

"The Ligurian diamond is on display today," she answered in her heavy Bronx accent before going back to her reading as if that explained everything.

Ligurian?

"I see. Thank you."

Alex had never heard of the Ligurian diamond. She had heard of the Hope diamond and she'd seen pictures of the British crown jewels, but that was about the extent of her knowledge of the world's most famous diamonds. As far as she was concerned, diamonds were synonymous with tragedy. The diamonds from six husbands hadn't brought her mother any happiness. To Alex's mind they represented the ashes of the mother-and-daughter relationship that had never happened.

She approached one of the security men at the door. When she explained that she had an appointment with the head jeweler, Mr. Defore, the guard made a quick phone call. A minute later he allowed her inside, where another guard escorted her through an installed metal detector.

When the beep went off, she was asked to open her purse and overnight bag.

Once he was satisfied with the search, she was free to continue with the other guard. As they moved to the elevator past yet some other guards keeping a close eye on the orderly crowd, she glimpsed a dark, teardrop-shaped diamond on display in the center of the elegant foyer. The dazzling stone had been placed on a brilliantly lit pedestal within a closed glass casing, but she was too far away to determine its color. No doubt a diamond of such a large size would easily pay her mother's debt.

The guard joined her inside the elevator. "Mr. Defore's office is on the second floor," he explained, drawing her attention back to the business at hand. When the doors opened again, he guided her to a suite on the right of the bank of elevators. A secretary in the reception area told her to sit down. Five minutes later Alex was shown in to Mr. Defore's private office.

"Come in, Ms. Grigory. You're right on time. I hope you had a pleasant flight from Los Angeles."

"I did. Thank you, Mr. Defore."

"Sit down over here." The short, pleasant-faced jeweler held out a chair for her, then went around the desk to his swivel chair to face her. "Coffee? Tea? A soft drink?"

"No, nothing, thank you. When Mr. Watkins made this appointment for me, we didn't realize you would have a diamond exhibit going on."

He smiled. "Once a year the Principality of Castelmare allows it to be on loan here for a day."

Castelmare, ruled by King Vittorio, had replaced Monaco as the favorite vacation destination on the Riviera for the world's most rich and famous. The former city-state was located on the Mediterranean where her mother had spent part of her sixth honeymoon.

"Do you know if the diamond will be on display in California?" Alex's boss would definitely want to see it.

Mr. Defore cocked his head. "It won't. Except for a yearly one-day showing in New York, London, Rio, Sydney, Hong Kong and Dubai, it stays in Castelmare."

Alex reflected that Rodeo Drive in L.A. was supposed to have some of the most exclusive shops in North America, but apparently not exclusive enough. "The House of Savoy is very fortunate to have been chosen to display it."

His brows lifted. "I don't think you understand, Ms. Grigory. The present day king of Castelmare is the latest Italian sovereign of the ancient House of Savoy. This store is the monarchy's property."

She blinked. "I had no idea."

No wonder her mother had been so ecstatic over the diamond bracelet her father had purchased here. Alex was indebted to Mr. Watkins for directing her to this store, where she would almost certainly get the highest price for the stones to pay off her mother's horrendous debts.

"Shall I take a look at your mother's collection now?"

His question jerked Alex from her torturous thoughts. "Of course." She opened the overnight bag and placed the jewel case on his desk, positioning it for Mr. Defore to open it himself. Mr. Defore nodded and got to work. Alex had never seen all her mother's jewelry before, only heard about it. She'd put the inventory from the bank in her purse. It listed seven diamond rings, four pairs of diamond earrings, one diamond bracelet, three diamond necklaces and two diamond ankle bracelets.

When he finally lifted the lid, the sight of the diamonds

would have impressed anyone except Alex, who simply mourned the life she'd never had with her mother. Money had been her mother's God, and Alex wondered how one person could have been so devoid of motherly instinct and could have demonstrated so much bad judgment in everything she did?

Mr. Defore said nothing as he began his examination. Because the House of Savoy dealt regularly with the world's wealthiest people, Alex realized her mother's possessions would cause no great stir. Certainly this jeweler had little interest in Kathryn Carlisle and simply got to work studying each piece with his loupe.

He finally lifted his head. Wearing a distinct frown he said, "Who told you these were diamonds?"

Caught off guard by the stunning question, Alex took a moment before she could recover enough to say, "Mr. Watkins, my mother's attorney."

The man shook his head. "These are imitations."

What?

Alex reeled, causing her to clutch the edge of the desk for support. "But that's impossible!"

"Perhaps she kept the real jewels in another case?"

She swallowed hard. There was no other case. "This was the only one in the bank vault," she whispered.

"I'm very sorry, Ms. Grigory. We deal with mined diamonds, not fabrications. I'm sure there are shops in Los Angeles that would pay twenty, maybe twenty-five hundred dollars for this assortment of costume jewelry."

"Surely you're joking!" During the flight she'd begun to get excited about being able to pay off the last of the huge debt whose weight felt like a stone sitting in the pit of her stomach.

"I assure you I'm not. Scientists have synthesized and created diamond alternatives meant to trick the naked eye. However, when you view them through the loupe, they haven't the fire or brilliance."

She shot out of the chair, too shaken to sit still. "Is there someone else I could speak to about this?"

A dull red entered his cheeks. "I'm the head jeweler here."

His rigid attitude prompted her to reach in the case and lift out a piece. "My father, Oleg Grigory, my mother's first husband, bought this diamond bracelet *here* twenty-six years ago. He was the owner of one of the largest casinos in Las Vegas. Surely you have a record of it somewhere, if only so I can verify it."

"One moment," he said quietly. "I'll research it on the computer."

She was shaking so hard from shock, she could hardly sit still while she waited.

"Yes. He did make such a purchase." His gaze switched to hers. "But I'm afraid it was not *that* bracelet. Perhaps your mother sold her jewels without telling anyone and had these replicas made to wear?"

Is that what you did, Mother? Did you sell your diamonds along with your soul? The possibility pierced her like a fiery metal shaft.

Taking a deep breath, she said, "I'd still like another opinion. Who's the manager of the House of Savoy?"

"Mr. Bernard Hudson. I'm afraid he's occupied with the showing of the Ligurian diamond."

"Will you tell him these are Kathryn Carlisle's jewels? When he learns of this situation, I know he'll want to talk to me." By now Alex was desperate enough to use her mother's name for leverage.

"You don't understand. He won't be available until tomorrow. I'll ask my secretary to make you an appointment with him."

"Surely he can spare five minutes? I'll wait."

"Impossible. Now I'm very sorry, Ms. Grigory, but I'm afraid you'll have to leave my office because I have other clients to see." He shut the case, leaving her holding the bracelet.

Her body tautened. "Look, Mr. Defore…I flew all the way from Los Angeles for this appointment. My return flight is booked for tonight." Her hand tightened around the bracelet, which according to him was nothing more than paste. "By tomorrow I'll be back on the West Coast. I have to talk to him!"

She fought not to lose her temper in front of this composed jeweler, who was probably paid an indecent sum of money not to lose his.

"At the risk of repeating myself, Ms. Grigory, there's nothing more I can do for you at present."

"Your manager has to eat lunch sometime today. Since he's on the premises, I can't believe he wouldn't take out a moment to see me."

"I'm sorry." The jeweler was implacable.

"What kind of a man are you?" she cried out in torment. "You can at least call him on the phone. Tell him who I am. Inform him this is a matter of life and death!" Without hesitation she grabbed the phone on his desk and held the receiver in front of him.

Maybe it was the fact that her five-foot-nine height gave her the advantage over him, or possibly it was the narrowing of her eyelids with their slightly tilted shape. Whatever the explanation, he finally took the receiver from her, but then hung it up.

Out of the corner of her eye she saw his hand move to press a button on his console. He was probably summoning security. So be it. Alex had come to New York on a mission.

Alex's mother had once accused her of being incredibly stubborn like her father. She'd been born Alexandra Carlisle Grigory. The one picture she had of her father showed him to be a tall man who'd died when Alex was just nine months old. Like her mother's death, the police still hadn't determined if his was accidental or staged to look like one.

The few people who knew she was Kathryn Carlisle's only offspring remarked that she must have inherited her father's genes. Michelle had once told her, "Your father gave you great bones, and your eyes are exactly the same gray as Greta Garbo's—you could be her double!" Nevertheless, Alex and her mother had been as different as apples and bananas.

Kathryn had been of medium height, and curvy. On or off the set, the platinum-blond bombshell had been the ultimate drama queen.

Alex on the other hand had unruly dark blond hair with nothing remarkable about her looks, even though Manny, like Michelle, had also insisted there was a similarity between her and Garbo. Alex had laughed off both their comments. They might think she looked like a film star, but Alex preferred to work behind the scenes where she transformed other people who acted in front of the camera.

Selfishly neglected by her mother and tragically deprived of the father she never knew, Alex had learned to function on her own from an early age. She had no extended family, but did have a few close friends that she could rely on. However, no one understood the extent of her grief, or her shame....

The pitiful legacy from both her parents had left a burning stain on Alex's soul. Now the questions surrounding her mother's death had left new scars on Alex, whose conception, according to her mother, had been a mistake from the beginning.

Kathryn Carlisle had been a film-star idol. She had been like a brilliant comet who had swept in and out of her daughter's existence once every millennium for only brief moments without an atom of motherly love. Alex had been raised by a trail of nannies from the age of three weeks old, and there'd been no anchor in her life except for Betty, the nanny who had taken a liking to her and who had introduced her to Michelle, head of the makeup department at one of the film studios.

When Alex had been set adrift physically and financially by her mother when she turned eighteen, Betty had been instrumental in getting her her first job in the makeup department. Alex had started off just helping out at first, but then over the years she had continued to work there while she attended college and after.

Michelle had said she was a fast learner with a natural talent. In time she paid a salary that allowed Alex to get a modest apartment and take care of herself. After her apprenticeship, Michelle had asked Alex to stay on. Lately she had hinted that she planned to give Alex more responsibility and a raise.

Alex was grateful, of course, and she'd never want to hurt Michelle's feelings, but she'd always had a dream of doing something else. Tragically it seemed out of reach now that she was saddled with her mother's debts and needed to find a fast way to pay for them.

Surely Mr. Defore had made a mistake, or the bank hadn't realized there were two jewel cases in the vault. One way or another Alex would straighten things out. It would be too excruciatingly painful to go home without the money.

She simply couldn't do it.

While the thirty-four-year-old crown prince of Castelmare sat in the security room of the House of Savoy chatting quietly with Carlo, one of his bodyguards, other local security guards manned the monitors of the twenty-four-hour surveillance cameras. They'd been strategically placed around the store to watch for anything out of the ordinary.

This stop in New York represented the last leg of a long trip that had taken Lucca around the world on business for his country. Unfortunately, he had no more excuses to stay away from Castelmare. The dreaded reunion with his parents was coming and inevitable. When he returned home this time, there'd be no escape from certain matters that would change his life forever.

Suddenly his attention was caught by the American woman he could see in the monitor. She was obviously upset, and he found himself listening intently. It seemed there was a situation developing in Defore's office.

Lucca's ears picked up the word Grigory, a name associated with the old Russian aristocracy. Curious, he turned to one of the computers and logged into several Web sites including the store's archives.

When he found what he wanted to know, he moved closer to the monitor with its black-and-white screen. That's when he heard another exchange that gave him pause. The woman battling with the head jeweler was Kathryn Carlisle's daughter?

He was stunned because he didn't know the Hollywood film idol even had children—he could see no physical resemblance.

Like all hot-blooded Italian males, Lucca appreciated a beautiful woman. He'd seen one of the star's films several years ago during a flight to Asia. The tempestuous actress, whose life had come to a tragic end like all too many American A-list celebrities, *did* have exceptional looks with her come-hither blue eyes and champagne-blond hair. Yet it appeared the only thing she'd passed on to her off-spring was her legendary, impossible temperament. Like mother, like daughter.

Defore didn't make mistakes. For that exact reason Lucca had appointed him to be head jeweler three years ago. Naturally he couldn't help but be fascinated by the woman's refusal to take Defore at his word. Evidently she was as spoiled as her mother and even more naive.

How could her daughter not have known the troubled star with her uncontrollable hunger for money would have run through her own finances a long time ago and had hocked her jewels as a last resort?

When the security alarm sounded, one of the guards said he'd take care of the problem and started for the door, but Lucca moved his six-foot-three frame out of the chair and reached it ahead of him.

"I'll deal with it." As he left the room with Carlo, he nodded to his other bodyguard standing outside the door. The three of them walked down the hall to Defore's office.

"Wait for me and don't let anyone else in," he told them both before opening the door. Once inside, he told the wide-eyed secretary she could take a long lunch, then he entered Defore's office.

The jeweler took one look at Lucca and was so shocked to see him rather than one of the security guards, he was struck dumb. Lucca had never had reason to interfere with Defore while he was working with a client, but then, he'd never been this intrigued before.

"I'll take over," he murmured, freeing a worried-looking Defore so he could leave. Lucca gave a barely perceptible shake of his head, warning the jeweler not to give him away.

"Yes, yes. Of course."

Lucca shut the door behind him before turning to face the flushed woman whose tall, willowy figure hadn't been noticeable from watching the screen. "Signorina Grigory?" He extended his hand.

After a slight hesitation she held on in a firm grip before releasing it. "I'm embarrassed Mr. Defore had to call in security, but all I wanted was to speak to Mr. Hudson for a minute," sounded a tearful voice she didn't try to hide.

He in turn didn't bother to correct her faulty assumption that he was part of the security team. In fact, he was glad of it, since it didn't happen very often that he wasn't recognized. The photos and lies perpetuated in the tabloids about Castelmare's playboy prince made anonymity virtually impossible no matter the continent where he traveled to do business for the crown.

Right now he was fascinated by her slightly windblown, dark blond hair and her lack of self-awareness. To his surprise there was nothing fake about her. Somehow he hadn't expected Kathryn Carlisle's daughter to be her total opposite in every way.

She was dressed in a draped, smoky-blue blouse tucked

into pleated beige pants, putting him in mind of a 1940s style. Only a woman of grace with long elegant legs, soft curves and square shoulders could get away with it.

This close he could see shadows beneath her pewter-gray eyes with their sweeping dark lashes. Lines caused by suffering bracketed her wide, voluptuous mouth, one of the few physical traits she'd inherited from her infamous mother.

The other familiar trait was less definable. She had a certain breathlessness bequeathed to her by her mother who'd exhibited that same quality on the screen. In person it created an air of urgency Lucca found exceptionally distracting.

"You said this was a matter of life and death?"

She tossed her head back nervously. "Yes," she blurted, "b-but I didn't realize our whole conversation had been captured on camera," she stammered. "Evidently you heard every word of it."

He shrugged. "A necessary precaution in this business." She eventually nodded. "Why don't we both sit down."

"Thank you." She returned to the chair opposite the desk. "I didn't mean to take you away from your duties when you have the responsibility of helping keep an eye on the Ligurian diamond display."

Lucca hadn't expected her to be this polite. Now that she was in control he found her low, husky voice incredibly attractive.

"It's under heavy guard. I'm not worried." He noticed she was still torturing the bracelet in her hand. "May I see it, please? Everyone hired by the House of Savoy is trained to recognize a mined diamond from a fake." Which was true.

As she handed it to him, their fingers brushed. Strange that he would be so aware of her he could still feel the sensation while he examined the stones beneath the loupe.

After a moment he said, "I'm afraid Mr. Defore was right. This bracelet is pure imitation. Dare I say not even a good one?"

The second he saw her face lose color, he moved to the corner of the room where he switched off the camera and the audio so they would have complete privacy.

"But my fath—"

"Your father *did* purchase a bracelet exactly like this years ago. I checked the records. It was valued at $500,000.00 back then and would probably be worth several million today."

Her expressive face crumpled. Alex knew that her mother had always kept certain secrets from her daughter. Yet this one had been quite a secret, since the whole collection would have brought her a nice sum of money if the stones had been genuine diamonds.

"I'm sorry, *signorina*." After the sensational headlines built up in the tabloids concerning her mother's lifestyle, he suspected the star hadn't been in control of her spending and had been forced to sell off her diamonds upon running into dire straits. It was a story that came out of Hollywood and circulated throughout Europe all too often.

He heard a despairing cry before a shadow crossed over her features. Then she buried her face in her hands. The sound of it found its way to his gut.

"Do you know if her jewelry was ever insured?"

A minute passed. Eventually she regained her composure and lifted her head. Her creamy complexion had gone splotchy again. "If it was, her attorney didn't know about it."

"I realize this news has come as a blow."

"A blow?" Her cry resonated in the room. "You have no idea— I *must* find a way to pay off her debts. I'd planned on this money. It was my last resort," her voice throbbed.

"Do you have a husband who would help out?"

"No." She looked away. "After my mother's track record, I have no interest in marriage," came the bitter response.

"I see." One could hardly blame her. "What about a lover?"

Her hands gripped the arms of the chair in what looked like a death grip. "Even if I did have one and he had the funds, I would never ask that of him."

Unaccountably moved by her vehement declaration he said, "Do you have any siblings?"

Her eyes closed for a second. "No. I'm her only child."

An only child so well hidden Lucca hadn't known of it. "Did she leave the diamonds to you in her will?" If Signorina Grigory had relied on this jewelry as her only hope of money after her mother's death, it would explain her shock.

"No," came the wooden reply. "She didn't make a will."

Lucca rubbed the back of his neck absently. Kathryn Carlisle with all her doomed marriages to wealthy men hadn't had the foresight to provide for her daughter? He wasn't able to comprehend it. "Why?"

"Why?" she repeated, staring at him through dull eyes. "That's like asking why she didn't abort when she found out she was pregnant with me. I came into her world unplanned and unwanted. She never publicly acknowledged me. Most of the time she forgot I was alive. It's all right. I learned life's lessons early, but I must admit I'm devastated about this."

She held up the bracelet he'd given back to her. "The money from her diamonds was supposed to pay what was left owing to salvage her reputation. I wanted the slate wiped clean so the creditors would go away once and for all. It's bad enough having to live with the terrible things people say about her, however true.

"I guess I hoped that if her bills got paid, it would be the one thing the world couldn't castigate her for. Her agent has every right to be paid what's owing him. I'm sick about it, that's all."

He inhaled heavily. "How much did she leave owing?"

"Twelve million dollars."

Not exactly small change. "What about your father? I realize they've been divorced for a long time, but would he consider covering part of it, if only for your sake?" The Grigory family would still have hidden resources.

"No," she answered without hesitation.

"Does he know about your situation?"

One graceful eyebrow lifted sardonically. "If he does, it's too late. He died before I was a year old. In fact, three of her husbands are dead. I have no idea what's happened to the other three."

Hearing the bald facts about the six-times-divorced actress made him wish he hadn't brought up the subject.

"Have you no extended family? Grandparents on your mother's side perhaps?" Lucca's world was filled with both.

"No. Mother was an orphan."

He rubbed his lower lip with his thumb. "Is there no property left to sell?"

She smiled, but it didn't reach her expressive eyes. "None. Except for the footage of her films, which I don't own, there's nothing left to prove she ever inhabited this world. The police lieutenant who investigated her death still hasn't ruled out suicide.

"No matter how estranged my mother and I were from day one, I didn't want to believe she was capable of taking her own life." After a silence she whispered, "Now I'm certain she did."

The break in her voice found a spot in Lucca's psyche that haunted him.

In the next instant she put the bracelet inside the jewelry case and shut it. "Will you please ask Mr. Defore to dispose of this and everything in it? I don't want to see it again and know I can rely on him for his discretion."

Before he could countenance it, she shoved it toward him. "Thank you for being so decent about this. You could've had me arrested. Please tell Mr. Defore I'm sorry for having a breakdown in front of him. He was very civilized and should be given a raise for his composure."

"I'll convey the message."

"I appreciate it. Though I hate to admit it, the dark side of the Carlisle in me comes out from time to time. The truth is, for good or evil I *am* part Carlisle. No matter how much I'd like to, I can't run away from my destiny."

Her words shook Lucca to the foundations. He felt like someone had just walked over his grave.

Tears dripped down her cheeks, but she didn't seem to be aware of it. "Do you know I've been sitting here calculating how long it will take me to pay back her debt so that I can restore some good to the Carlisle name?" She made a little sound of despair. "I don't know what the House of Savoy pays its security guards, but if I can eke out $500.00 a month—which is all I can afford on my present salary, it will only take me 2,000 years to wipe out the debt."

Her pain-filled laugh bordered on hysteria, but considering her fierce disappointment, he could well understand the display of raw emotion.

She jumped up from the chair and closed her overnight bag. "I'm the world's biggest fool not to know these jewels were as fake as the life she led. Forgive me for venting in front of you like this—I've probably said too much already." Before he could countenance it, her regal-like strides had taken her halfway across the room, leaving a trail of peach scent behind.

"Come back and sit down, Signorina Grigory. I'm not through with you." He knew his voice had sounded peremptory just now, but it was an acquired trait he couldn't seem to help any more than he could stop breathing.

She whirled around white-faced. "So, you *are* going to have me charged with unruly conduct. My mistake."

Lucca stared at her for a long moment. "Nothing could be further from the truth," his voice grated. The sadness she'd encountered in her life made him want to shield her from any more. "You haven't done anything wrong. What I would like to do is talk to you further about your situation."

Even from the distance separating them he could see her body tauten. "Why? It's no one else's business but mine. If you were hoping for an autographed photo of my mother, I'm afraid I don't have one and never did."

How tragic her first assumption was all tangled up with Kathryn Carlisle's effect on men. He got to his feet. "What I have on my mind has nothing to do with your mother. Since I was willing to listen to you, I would hope you would grant me the same courtesy."

There was a fight going on inside of her. He'd appealed to her sense of fair play while he waited for her capitulation. "I have a solution to your problem," he said to add weight.

She let out an incredulous laugh. "*You* have a solution. Does that mean you can arrange for me to win the lottery?"

"In a manner of speaking," he came back. His response managed to erase the mocking expression from her features. "However, I'd prefer it if we were seated to discuss it. Shall we start over again?"

Caught on the horns of a dilemma, she didn't advance or retreat. She needed help. He intended to give it to her.

"Before we go any further, let me introduce myself. My name is Lucca Umberto Schiaparelli Vittorio V."

CHAPTER TWO

ALEX studied the black-haired male who'd been in-terrogating her all this time. The second he'd walked in to Mr. Defore's office wearing a light gray, hand-tailored silk suit that molded his powerful frame to perfection, he'd no more looked, talked or acted like a security guard than fly!

He was too well bred, too sophisticated. His faintly ac-cented English had polish. Combined with his aristocratic bearing, she hadn't been able to put him in any kind of a slot. There was much more to him than the fact that he was a tall, darkly handsome, olive-skinned Italian—in truth, the most attractive man she'd ever met in her life.

Now that she knew who he was, she realized she'd seen pictures of him flashed across the screen. She'd never paid much attention for the very fact that her mother had always gone for the larger-than-life types, just like Lucca. Anyone the media had hyped Alex chose to ignore.

In the flesh, the crown prince of Castelmare defied the normal adjectives one would apply to a good-looking man. There weren't enough in the English language to do justice to his charisma.

With the Ligurian diamond on display, it was no coinci-dence he was here in New York. Undoubtedly he'd brought the famous stone to the States via the monarchy's private plane.

This was her unlucky day. No man or woman had ever seen her this vulnerable before.

"You lied to me," she accused him hotly.

"If you mean I didn't correct your assumption that I was a security guard, then I have to plead guilty."

"Does the royal Riviera playboy make it a regular practice to impersonate the hired help?" His dark eyes with their jet-black lashes suddenly took on a strange glitter that lent heat to her growing anger. "Or was it on a whim you decided to amuse yourself by toying with Kathryn Carlisle's daughter while she poured out her guts? Either way, congratulations. You've made my humiliation doubly complete."

Burning with rage, she turned on her heel and fled to the next room, but she was stopped at the outer door by an unsmiling, robust, Italian secret-service type planted there.

Naturally the prince wouldn't make a move without all his bets being covered. She shut the door in the bodyguard's face and wheeled around. Her nemesis lounged against the doorjamb of Mr. Defore's office with his strong arms folded, insolently at ease.

More infuriated than ever, she said, "Am I to assume *you're* the lottery, as long as I provide certain services? Would it give you some kind of perverted rush to claim you slept with Kathryn Carlisle's daughter?" An angry laugh escaped as she shook her head. "You *must* be hard up for new thrills to consider handing over twelve million dollars to me, but unlike my mother, my body's not for sale at any price!"

Undaunted he said, "I'm glad to hear it. Lovely as your body is, I'm not asking for it. However, I *am* in need of something else you could give me that would solve the most serious problem of my life…and yours. Come back in and sit down while we talk about it. This could take a while."

"I can't imagine being able to offer anything that would solve your problem…whatever it is."

"You'd be surprised," came the cryptic comment. "Give me half an hour of your time."

She shook her head. "I'm sorry. I have to be at the airport later today and don't have time to spare."

He gazed at her intently. "Not even if the result of our meeting might mean clearing your mother's debts once and for all? When I heard you cry out earlier that this was a matter of life and death, it sounded like you meant it."

Alex studied him without averting her eyes. "I did."

She heard his deep intake of breath. "What if I told you I have a situation that's a matter of life and death for me, too. Would that make a difference to you?"

What was she supposed to say to such a question? Something in his tone led her to believe he might be telling the truth. Incredible how he'd turned things around so she felt guilty if she didn't at least listen to what he had to say.

"I'll give you five minutes."

"Thank you. Come back inside the other room."

Against her better judgment she did his bidding and retraced her steps. As she sat down, he spoke in Italian to someone on the phone before he took his place across from her. Then he typed something on the computer and printed it out.

Handing it to her, he said, "Your mother was married to royalty, did you know that?"

"Mother was married to four men with supposed titles,

but in time those claims turned out to be false. Everything about her life was a sham."

He eyed her narrowly. "Except that your father was the real thing."

"You mean, a Las Vegas racketeer."

"Rumors have a lot to answer for, particularly when they're founded in jealousy and greed. Read what's on the paper. You should find the information of the greatest interest."

Alex looked down:

After the October Revolution of 1917 all classes of the Russian nobility were legally abolished. Many members of the Russian nobility who fled Russia after the Bolshevik Revolution played a significant role in the white emigré communities that settled in Europe, in North America and in other parts of the world.

In the 1920s and 1930s, several Russian nobility associations were established outside Russia, including groups in France, Belgium and the United States. By 1938, the Russian Nobility Association in New York was founded. Since the collapse of the Soviet Union, there has been a growing interest among Russians in the role the Russian nobility played in their historical and cultural development.

Membership is exclusively reserved to persons who are listed in the nobility archives. Those titled members are recorded below with their former titles, genealogies and photos available.

Alex scanned the list until her gaze fell on the name Grigory. She gasped softly when she saw the last name on the Grigory royal family tree. It read "Prince Oleg

Rostokof Grigory, son of Prince Nicholas Grigory and Princess Vladmila Rostokof, born in New York, 1958, now living in Las Vegas, Nevada."

Her heart clapped like thunder as she looked at a picture of her handsome, dark blond father, who couldn't be more than eighteen in this picture. The strong physical resemblance between daughter and father at that age was uncanny.

As her head flew back, a security guard entered and brought them two sodas. After he left, the prince pushed one toward her and took a lengthy swallow from the other. When he put it down again, he said, "Where did you get the idea that your father was part of the underworld?"

"One of my nannies mentioned that she'd heard my father was involved with the Russian mafia. As I grew older and realized what that meant, I was ashamed and frightened by the possibility. I hid away in case one of them tried to find me and hurt me. My repulsion over my mother's ghastly lack of judgment in marrying him was so severe I didn't want to know anything more about him.

"By the time she'd gone through her sixth divorce, so many preposterous tales were circulating about her and her past husbands, I couldn't handle it and tried to shut it out. To my horror the police came to my work and told me she'd died of what looked like too much alcohol mixed with drugs. At that point it was too late to ever ask her what the truth was. I'm not sure she would have told me anyway." Her voice shook.

He finished the rest of his soda. "You've been through a great deal of pain in your life. Nothing can wipe that away, but the sooner her bills are paid, the sooner you can start to concentrate on other things."

A fresh spurt of anger filled her system. She looked back

at her father's picture. "Are you saying I should do something as crass and ignoble as turn to my father's family for
the money? Is *that* what you're suggesting? A modern-day
Anastasia story with an ugly twist?" she said. Her shrill
voice reverberated in the room's confines.

"Not at all," came his bland reply, exasperating her even
more. "But it might be of some comfort to you to get acquainted with the extended family you've never met or
known. Your grandparents are no longer alive, but your
great-uncle Yuri Grigory, is still living and has an apartment
here in New York. I met him a year ago at an embassy function. I can arrange for you two to get acquainted."

Alex was so stunned by what he'd just told her she didn't
know what to say. Realizing she needed to get hold of herself, she drank half of her soda without taking a breath.

The news about her father's lineage had come as a total
shock. Mafia or not, it appeared he did descend from a
royal background, otherwise the crown prince of
Castelmare wouldn't have been able to produce the
evidence she held in her hand.

Puzzled and confused by this whole experience, she eyed
him warily. "If you hoped this information would help give
me a sense of identity, I…I appreciate it." Her voice faltered.
"However, I still fail to understand where this conversation
is headed. What does any of this have to do with you?"

He sat forward, impaling her with his midnight-brown
eyes. She'd thought at first they were black. "My life has
been the opposite of yours. I was raised in a happy home
with loving parents, a loving sister, a large extended family
on all sides and good friends. Everything has been ideal
except for one glaring obstacle that has driven a wedge between my father and me."

"You mean, he wants you to give up your wicked, worldly bachelor ways and marry the princess he's had picked out for you from birth."

After a pause, "I can see you've heard this story before."

"One of my nannies read *Cinderella* to me. I didn't like it."

He cocked his dark head. "Why not?"

"When Cinderella's mother died, she had to be raised by a cruel stepmother. I thought it was an awful story, probably because I felt like my mother had died. In fact, it was much worse because I knew she was alive, but she never wanted to be with me."

The glimmer of compassion in his eyes forced her to look away. Once more she was embarrassed to have been caught baring her soul to this man who was a perfect stranger to her. The prince of Castelmare no less. "I always hated fairy tales after that."

"Then you and I have something in common," he muttered in his deep-toned voice. "When my mother read *Cinderella* to my sister and me, I hated it, too, because I wasn't a normal little boy who could grow up to do what I wanted. I was a prince, and my father was the king. Because I loved him, I knew that one day I'd have to do what he wanted and marry a princess who was ugly and mean and whom I'd despise."

Once the words sank in, Alex burst into laughter. She couldn't help it. What had started out as a strange, surreal conversation between the two of them had taken on something that went beneath the surface and resonated.

After her amusement faded there was an awkward silence before she said, "I've seen some of the princesses you've been with in the news and know for a fact they're beautiful. Whether they're mean or not, I have no idea, but none of the photos would convince me you despised them. Far from it," she added pointedly.

He sat back in the swivel chair. "You're right, of course. Several of my parents' royal favorites are charming, lovely and I think genuinely kind. However, I have a little problem because I've never been attracted to them."

"Just to the nonroyals."

For a moment a bleakness entered his eyes tugging at her emotions, then it vanished as if it had never been. "What was it your George Washington said? I cannot tell a lie." The prince had too much charm for his own good. "Have you ever had that problem with a man?" he asked, studying her features rather intently. "He has all the right qualities, but he doesn't speak to your soul?"

All the time, Alex muttered inwardly. "Errol Flynn was the only man who became my fantasy. When I saw him in *Robinhood,* I asked my nanny to take me again and again. We saw it twenty-five times."

It was his turn to laugh, the full-bodied male kind she felt to her toes. "I understand he still has a habit of speaking to every woman's soul, even from beyond the grave."

She nodded. "Some men are like that. Bigger than life." Alex realized she was looking at one of them.

"Bigger than life," his voice trailed. "A sort of chemistry of the body and spirit, wouldn't you say?"

"Yes," she whispered. This was no shallow prince, let alone man.

"That's what I'd hoped to find before now in the royal pickings, but it hasn't happened."

Alex had never given much thought to a problem like his until this minute. She was glad she wasn't in his royal shoes because she knew herself too well and could never marry anyone for the sake of duty. Perish the thought of being tied to someone you didn't love with your whole heart and soul.

Obviously, her mother hadn't had the capacity to truly love anything or anyone except herself. Sometimes it frightened Alex to think that because she was her daughter, she might have inherited that same inability to be devoted to one man.

There'd been boyfriends, but Alex hadn't yet suffered that grand passion her mother had managed to portray on the screen instead of real life. Maybe Alex never would. Aware something was expected of her, she said, "That could change in time. Some royal princess could come into your life you've overlooked. How old are you?"

"Thirty-four."

Nine years older than herself.

"That's still relatively young."

"From my point of view I agree, but my parents had hoped I'd be married by twenty-five and a father by twenty-six. To quote my mother, 'For you to be thirty-four and still single is positively indecent, Lucca. The whole country is waiting.'"

The way he imitated his parent made Alex chuckle. "At least your mother cares about you and loves you."

"She does, but there's more to it than that. My father's not well and needs to step down. It's within my power to lengthen his days by becoming king, thus relieving him of all responsibilities, but I can't become his successor without first taking a wife. Those are the rules.

"As a way of playing on my guilt, my mother and sister continually remind me I'm the only son and the only one who can perform this duty to save the day."

And Alex had thought *she'd* lived with a burden all these years.

She smoothed an errant curl away from her forehead. "What's wrong with your father?"

"He's had lung cancer."

"I'm sorry. How cruel to him and hard for all of you."

"It has been," the prince conceded, causing her to feel an empathy for him she didn't want to feel. "Part of his right lung was removed, leaving him in a weakened condition. Though he's in remission, the doctor says this disease is tenacious and it's only a matter of time before it comes back. The best medicine for him would be to give up the throne and relax."

Alex cleared her throat. "Since you love him so much, it seems you don't have a choice. Is there someone from the royal pickings you believe cares for you enough that you could see yourself married to her?"

"I can't answer that question since I haven't given them much of a chance to get to know me. The thought of marriage to any of them is something I can't abide."

Well, Alex. Ask a foolish question…

There was one princess Lucca had known for several years. Neither he nor Sofia were romantically involved, but they'd become good friends. Both sets of parents expected them to marry, but she wanted to abdicate her title and serve a humanitarian cause, thus allowing her younger sister to be the next in line. Sofia was waiting for Lucca to marry before she made the secret known to her family.

Out of loyalty to her and her wishes, he'd remained silent. Suddenly restless, he got up from the chair. "I need to choose someone who understands the situation for exactly what it is. No lies. No self-deception or pretense."

"You mean, someone who has no expectation of love. Is there such a woman?"

"Among my parents' short list? No." Except for Sofia. Sofia who devoted her life to charity work in Africa and had a missionary zeal to help people.

He came to sit on the corner of the desk so his legs brushed hers. "But an extraordinary thing happened to me today. I've met someone who would be the perfect consort to come to my rescue in this emergency situation. At the same time I could help her in ways no one else can. She's of royal blood yet is under no illusions about life or me. Better yet, she's single and uninvolved with a man at present."

As the portent of his words sank in, Alex's eyes widened in disbelief. What he'd just intimated was so outrageous, an odd sound escaped her lips. She slid out of the chair to put distance between them.

"You *are* out of your mind and can't possibly mean what you're saying."

He rose to his intimidating height. "I never say what I don't mean," came the words of steel. "When you get to know me better, you'll realize I've never been more serious about anything in my life."

She shook her head. "So you'll pay my mother's debts if I agree to marry you. Then you'll become king and two strangers will live unhappily ever after in a loveless marriage with no hope of producing an heir and both of us sneaking behind the scenes looking for fulfillment elsewhere."

He gave a careless shrug of his elegant shoulders. "If that's what you want."

Alex hugged her arms to her waist. "What I want doesn't come into it. This conversation is utterly absurd!

Don't you know that old movie script has been done and redone ad nauseum?"

One dark brow quirked. "But not to the tune of twelve million dollars. That will be my wedding present to you. In return, you'll play the loving wife in front of other people, be it my family or the public."

"I will not!"

"I've spent time with your great-uncle," he continued talking, unfazed by her outburst. "Do you know you have the same regal bearing? I noticed it immediately. The perfect plum from the royal Grigory tree."

She let out a strangled cry that was probably heard by everyone inside the House of Savoy.

"I meant that as a compliment, Alexandra."

The way he said her name just now with his slight Italian accent made her body tremble. That angered her further.

"However tarnished the sordid legacy from my mother, I'm not a piece of fruit to be plucked!"

His expression grew solemn. "No. Like a gift from the gods you've fallen into my hands at the providential moment to save us both from a hideous fate." —

Hideous was the word, all right. The thought of going back to Los Angeles to face her mother's creditors, to face poor Manny, let alone live with the smear tactics the media would always use against her caused bile to rise in her throat.

"I'm not asking that this arrangement last forever," he added in a velvety tone.

"Of course not. Just a lifetime," she blurted on a note of sarcasm.

One dark eyebrow dipped. "Who knows? Neither of us can see that far ahead into the future."

She bit her lip. "How inconvenient for you."

"You have no idea," his voice grated, conveying some deep-seated emotion that caught her on the raw.

"When is your wedding supposed to take place?"

"Preferably yesterday."

"Obviously." She tried to hide her smile but lost the struggle.

"To answer your question, my parents have planned it for a month from today. The wedding ceremony will follow my coronation in the cathedral."

Only four weeks? "I'm sure a royal wedding takes a great deal more time than that to organize."

"You don't know my parents. Everything's been arranged. It's only a matter of adding one detail…the name of the woman I've chosen. They've been living for this day."

"That's nice. I can't say the same thing about mine. Now I'm afraid I have to go. My job is waiting for me back in Los Angeles and I have a plane to catch." She started for the outer door once more.

"Is it your chosen career?"

When she reached it, she looked over her shoulder at him. "What? Putting makeup on movie stars? No. The job chose me and has kept me alive."

He moved closer. Her heart did a funny kick. "What job would you choose if you could?"

That gave her pause. "You mean, in my wildest dreams?"

It was his turn to chuckle. "Is it that out of the ordinary?"

"For me, yes."

"You want to be an astronaut?"

"No." Her mouth curved upward once more. "This is something very down-to-earth."

"What would that be?"

"It's as improbable as my meeting a real prince today."

"Why?"

"In the first place, I have to find a job where I can earn a lot of money in order to pay off mother's debts before I do anything else."

"And in the second place?" he queried.

"I don't know if I could make the grade."

"Doing what? Humor me," he prodded.

"Plastic surgery."

His intelligent gaze grew thoughtful. "Why that particular profession?"

"My mother was labeled the most beautiful woman in the world. Her love affair with herself was obscene. There are people out there born with facial problems who'd give everything they possessed to be able to look in the mirror and not cringe or grieve at the sight.

"If I could change one person's looks enough to make life more bearable for them, I'd give anything to do it."

A marked stillness pervaded the atmosphere before he spread his hands in a typical Italian gesture. "A noble aspiration. If that's your raison d'être, then make it a reality once we're married."

Maybe she was hallucinating.

"Why not?" He read her mind. "Castelmare University in Capriccio has a medical school linked with the University of Genoa."

The man was starting to get to her and that was frightening.

"Look—I was talking about my wildest dreams. The point is, not even *I* would want to be married to me. And lest you forget, one has to speak Italian to go to your university. For your information, I can only say one word in your language. It's *ciao*."

She opened the door to leave, but it was blocked by the same person as before. Another bodybuilder type was standing behind him. In the next breath she shut it again and turned on the man whose charisma was positively lethal. "Will you please tell Salvatore and his brother out there to let me pass?"

He let out a hearty laugh at her reference to the famous Italian bodyguard Salvatore Bartolotta, who lost his life trying to protect an antimafia prosecutor during the 1930s. While admiring his quick mind, Alex tried hard not to react to his full-bodied response. It made him appear younger and even more appealing. She hadn't thought it was possible.

"Carlo will be flattered when I tell him. You're obsessed by the mafia. Why is that, Alexandra? More than likely it was the mob that targeted your father because of his title and financial affluence. When he wouldn't cooperate, they rubbed him out. I believe that's the American term."

The prince knew it was. He was too intelligent by far.

"Wherever the truth lies, anyone linked to the mafia eventually dies like the father I never knew." She looked down. "I don't know why we're having this conversation. You've picked the wrong woman to help you out of your nightmare. I need to go home and face mine."

"I'm not prepared to let you go yet," he whispered silkily. "A little while ago you accused me of being hard up. That's putting it mildly. My back's up against the proverbial wall and my time has run out. I can't fly home and face my parents without producing the name of my intended bride. As I've told you, I've been overdue in that department for the past ten years."

She couldn't believe she was still standing here listening to him instead of banging on the door to demand her freedom.

"And you honestly believe they'll be overjoyed you've chosen the most unsuitable female on the planet to parade before your kingdom? Marriage to Kathryn Carlisle's daughter will make you the laughingstock of the civilized world."

"Let me worry about it."

"I'll do better than that. You won't have to be concerned about anything because my answer is no! Can you imagine what the media would make of it?

"In a shocking palace exclusive today, the bachelor crown prince of Castelmare has bypassed many a royal swan to choose the ugly duckling of the deceased, washed-up American film goddess Kathryn Carlisle for his bride.

"Rumors at court say the prince hasn't been himself since a golf ball hit him in the temple in Pebble Beach, California, where he was on hand for the U.S. Open with international supermodel Germaine."

His grin disarmed her. "You, of all people, should know better than to believe the tabloids. That ball hit one of my bodyguards in the knee. Any photo of a model was super-imposed for effect."

Her jaw hardened. "Where my mother was concerned, I *do* believe them. Don't forget they wrote the truth about her. Marrying you will give them enough fodder to start a whole new feeding frenzy.

"The headlines will read, 'With the promise of a twelve-million-dollar wedding present, it appears the daughter is following in the footsteps of the mother. Time will tell if this is the first of her many marriages destined to fail. Bets in the Las Vegas underworld are already running high that the marriage will fall apart within months.'"

Something flickered in the dark recesses of his eyes. "Then prove them wrong, Alexandra."

There he went again saying her name in that unusual way, making her nerve endings tingle. While blood surged into her cheeks, her hands formed fists. "Enough is enough! I could never take your money."

Lucca liked tangling with her. He'd finally met a woman who set off exhilarating sparks when they were together. He couldn't remember the last time this had happened.

"Fine. Then become a surgeon and pay back the debt with your hard-earned money. A few operations for those who can afford it and you'll have wiped your mother's slate clean as you indicated earlier."

Her chin lifted. "Even if by some miracle I did get in medical school, I wouldn't be able to start practicing for another eight years!"

"I'll pay for your medical school for as long as it takes. Once you do your residency, you'll receive a salary and can start paying me back like you would a school loan. It's a good bargain. I guarantee you couldn't do better with anyone else."

She stared at him through glazed eyes. "Attending medical school isn't one of the duties of a king's consort."

"My consort will do what she wants because I won't be a normal sort of king." He flashed her a self-satisfied smile. "Your only royal duties will be to accompany me on certain occasions that will come up from time to time."

"I see."

"I'll arrange for you to start Italian lessons tomorrow after we arrive at the palace. By the time we've returned from our honeymoon six weeks from now, the fall semester will be starting. With the help of a tutor, you'll be able to keep up with your fellow medical students."

"Perhaps you didn't hear me. I'm terrible at languages and I'm not going anywhere with you." Least of all on a honeymoon.

"When I explain your predicament with the American press, my parents will insist you live at the palace for the next month. Being sequestered with the family will protect you from the worst of the media for a while."

She felt like stomping both feet. "Aside from the fact that you're speaking pure nonsense, I can't just quit my job and leave my apartment!"

"We'll talk about that later." He checked his watch. "Right now we're going to meet your great-uncle. He's the deputy consul at the Russian Federation here in New York. When he finds out you're his brother's granddaughter, he'll be overjoyed and insist we meet to get acquainted."

The prince moved past her and opened the door where both his bodyguards were still standing on alert. With a hand cupping her elbow he said, "While you visit the ladies' room on your right, I'll make the arrangements.

"Don't take too long. There's a lot to accomplish before we board my private jet this evening. And one more thing. My name is Lucca. I'd like you to use it."

CHAPTER THREE

"YURI Pavlovich Grigory? May I present your grand-niece, Princess Alexandra Carlisle Grigory."

"Alexandra, my child." The tall, eighty-year-old widower with his strong Russian accent kissed her on both cheeks. "Welcome to the family."

"I can't believe I have living family," Alex whispered shakily, touched by his unexpected warmth. She was still incredulous any of this was happening. If it weren't for Lucca, she would never have been united with her father's family, let alone known of their existence.

Though she was indebted to him, she was also terrified because this reunion had come about at a price. There was only one way Lucca wanted repayment, but she couldn't do what he asked.

"There are quite a few of us Grigorys so you'll *have* to believe it." He chuckled. "Call me Uncle Yuri."

She blinked back the tears. "If you don't mind."

"Mind?" He shook his gray head. "I'd be hurt if you called me anything else. This is a great day. Do you know you're the living image of my nephew, except you're much prettier?" He squeezed her hand. "That's because of your mother. She and Oleg created a beautiful daughter." His eyes misted over. "If only your father and grandfather could see you."

"Thank you, Uncle Yuri. I'd give anything to have known them."

"Well—" He wiped his eyes. "I'll do my best to tell you all about them. Come into the conference room and we'll talk over lunch."

Lucca escorted her through the double doors to the other room where a meal was waiting for them. Over the next few hours her Uncle Yuri told her so many wonderful stories, the time flew by and she never wanted the afternoon to end. Between the pictures and anecdotes, she felt as if she really did belong to a great family.

Yuri's kindness about her mother made it easy for Alex to love him. So far he'd said nothing disparaging about her parent. It was like a balm to her scarred heart.

"First Vladmila, then Nicholas got pneumonia and died. Oleg left New York to figure out what he wanted to do with his life. Once he reached Las Vegas, I'm afraid he didn't keep in touch. We didn't hear until after the fact that he'd died in a plane crash. Such a young age to lose his life. I wish I'd known he had a daughter. To think you grew up in Los Angeles without him."

While she fought to control her tears, his moist gray eyes swerved in Lucca's direction. "My children and grandchildren will be surprised and thrilled to learn of Alexandra's existence. I have you to thank for uniting us, Lucca."

The prince sat there at ease, the quintessential picture of royal sophistication. "It was my pleasure, believe me."

"Whatever I can do to repay you, name it."

Alex felt Lucca's dark eyes on her and shivered, wondering what he was thinking. She didn't have to wait long to find out.

"I'm glad you said that because I've asked Alexandra to marry me." She gasped. "We hope to gain your blessing and would request that you do us the honor of giving her away at our wedding next month."

"Is this true?" Yuri cried. He looked delighted.

Her breath caught. "I…I haven't said yes yet, Uncle," she stumbled over the words.

"Why ever not?"

Alex wanted to blurt that they'd only met six hours ago, but she was too embarrassed to tell him the truth. Instead she said, "We haven't known each other very long."

Her great-uncle stared into her eyes. "That's what marriage is for, to get to know each other, my child. You'll have years of togetherness while you learn more and more how to make each other happy."

She moistened her lips nervously. "You don't understand, Uncle Yuri. My mother was married six times." Not to mention that before today Alex and Lucca had been total strangers. Marriages like this simply didn't happen.

"I can understand why you're frightened. But think about this." He lifted his forefinger as if he was giving a speech. "Maybe part of it's because she lost Oleg, and maybe the other part is because she didn't have parents to teach her what a good marriage is all about. Hmm?"

"Maybe," she answered in a tiny voice. He'd confounded her thoughts with his reasoning, and it didn't help that Lucca sat there looking pleased and impossibly confident.

"Don't forget you've got *me* now. My marriage to your great-aunt Natasha lasted sixty years. There's no reason yours won't last that long or longer!"

He was very sweet. She squeezed his hand back. Already a bond had developed, but he didn't have the faintest clue what was going on here. Alex felt as though she'd been caught up in a tornado and had no idea where it was carrying her.

"If Lucca has the good sense to choose a Grigory when there are other eligible royals who've had their eye on him for years, then I can guarantee a happy union. Our family stays faithful to each other."

Lucca sat forward, capturing her gaze. "For my part I intend to do everything to make you happy."

"There," her uncle cried out. "You see?"

Yes…she saw. What her uncle didn't know was that the most vital ingredient in their marriage would be missing, but she held back in deference to her newly found relative who was beaming. Too agitated to sit still, she reached for her coffee and drank it.

"Alexandra?" he said excitedly. "You're the loveliest of all the Grigory women. I noticed it when you walked in with Lucca. You two make a splendid match."

"I thought the same thing the first time I laid eyes on her," Lucca concurred with an unmistakable tone of sensuality.

Alex choked on the hot liquid and put the cup back on the saucer. He'd gauged it just right to convince her great-uncle he was in love. The crown prince of Castelmare was a sensational actor.

While she wiped the corner of her mouth with her napkin, Lucca got to his feet and went around to her chair. "I dislike cutting this meeting short, Yuri, but Alexandra and I have to leave for the airport."

This was Alex's cue to get up from the table. As she stood, their arms brushed. The contact sent a shockwave through her body. She hurried ahead while her great-uncle, who was as tall as Lucca, followed suit. He moved to the outer door of his office like a person ten years younger and kissed her on both cheeks.

"Lucca has my number. Let me know you've arrived safely in Castelmare. Now that we've met, I want the two of you to be part of my life, Alexandra."

Tears smarted her eyes. "I want that, too!" She gave him a big hug. "You'll never know what this day has meant to me."

"I think I do." He sniffed before handing her a manila envelope full of family pictures. His gaze shifted to Lucca. "Take good care of her. She's very precious to me."

To her shock Lucca put his arm around her shoulders. Dazzling her with his white smile, he said, "I intend to." It sounded more like a fierce avowal. "When the time comes, I'll send the jet for you and your family."

"That won't be necessary."

"I insist," Lucca stated in a tone of finality.

"Then we'll be waiting most impatiently." Yuri gave her a grandfatherly kiss on the forehead before Lucca whisked her through the door.

Paolo and Carlo, the bodyguards he'd introduced to her earlier were waiting to escort them out a rear exit. In the back alley three bullet-proofed limousines with smoked glass were parked. She had no idea who was inside the first one. Carlo followed them into the middle one. Paolo rode in the limo behind. Lucca sat next to her. Whether on purpose or not, his body rested against hers.

"You should never have said anything to my uncle. I haven't agreed to marry you. I don't even have a passport."

"I can let anyone I want into the country."

She gripped the armrest. With Lucca this close to her,

she couldn't think clearly. "Uncle Yuri thought you were serious about your marital intentions."

"I am. I wish I could convince you this is a good way out for both of us." An almost mournful quality had crept into his voice. "You gave me the impression you would do whatever it takes to pay the debt, even if it requires eight years at medical school to accomplish, but it appears I was wrong."

Alex edged against the door. "Everyone will say I'm just like my mother, running after a prince for his money."

"You're a princess in your own right and don't need anyone's money, but it doesn't matter what other people think," he came back suavely. "We're the only two people who know the truth or need to know."

She kneaded her hands. "We'd never be able to fool your parents," her voice throbbed.

"We don't have to. They're painfully aware I'll be struggling to do my duty, but it's expected."

Her thoughts reeled. "So there is a woman."

After a slight pause she heard him murmur yes.

Alex shouldn't have been surprised by his last-minute confession. He loved a woman with whom he could never share his life openly or marry. He couldn't have children with her, couldn't grow old with her. From the moment he was born, he'd been robbed of his free agency. How dreadful.

"No one else has knowledge of our situation, Alexandra, not even my sister, and she's my closest confidante. You're the only person who knows the truth."

She lowered her head. "I can't imagine your pain. I'm so sorry."

"I'm sorry your mother's debts have placed such an unbearable burden on you. We could help each other out, but if you can't bring yourself to do it, then I won't pressure you further."

Alex clasped her hands together, not having expected this kind of honesty from him. He was in love with someone. What could be more natural, except that he couldn't marry a commoner. When it got right down to it, how many men were honorable enough to sacrifice their personal happiness to this degree?

Earlier he'd indicated that his interest in women lay with nonroyals, but not until this second did she realize what exactly he was being forced to give up for the sake of his father's health and the kingdom.

No matter how hard Alex fought it, she felt a wrench in her heart for him. For the first time all day it didn't seem quite so ridiculous that he'd chosen Kathryn Carlisle's daughter of all people to carry off this charade. Through the backhand of fate she had enough Grigory royal blood in her veins to satisfy his parents. Lucca knew her darkest secrets. There would be no pretense between them in private, no surprises. She'd already told him she never planned to marry. There'd be no expectations of love on either side.

From her point of view she'd be getting the best of the bargain by being able to pursue her education toward a career. If she became a doctor, she would eventually pay him back. If she couldn't get into medical school, she'd find another career and pay him back. When that became a reality, she'd start paying off the twelve million dollars.

What would he get besides a titular wife?

Not much…unless she helped him find a way to be with the woman he loved. Now that would be worth something no one else could give him.

Alex could do that! She *wanted* to. It would even things up and they'd both get what they wanted.

"We're approaching the lane for the airport," he said, breaking in on her chaotic thoughts. "Tell me the terminal where your flight will be taking off so I can alert the driver."

Her pulse throbbed against her temples. By the timbre of his voice you'd never guess the turmoil going on inside of him, but she knew.

"What princess will you choose?"

"I have no idea. If we had more time I'd let you pick her for me. Somewhere over the Atlantic I'll have to make my choice. We're almost there. Where shall we drop you?"

She closed her eyes tightly. "You really want to go through with this?" It was a stupid question of course.

In the quiet that followed, his hand slid over her wrist. "Let's put it this way. I would never have come into Defore's office otherwise." While she digested that revelation he added, "If you're saying what I think you're saying, be very sure, Alexandra. There's no going back."

Her breath caught. "I know."

In the next instant he lifted her hand and kissed the palm. It set off a charge that ignited every atom of her body.

Lucca felt her quiver. She was frightened, but not too frightened to have agreed to his proposal. He'd counted on her desire to pay back her mother's debts being greater than any other consideration and she hadn't disappointed him. Later he would deal with his guilt over allowing her to think he was in love with Sofia. Right now his overriding emotion was one of exquisite relief bordering on triumph.

They drove the rest of the way in an electrifying silence he felt no compunction to break. She could change her mind at any moment. He wouldn't be able to relax until she was safely on board the jet and they'd attained cruising speed.

When Lucca was on business for the monarchy, he traveled with a staff of twelve, not including the pilot, copilot, steward or his bodyguards. By the time they reached the plane, everyone in his entourage had assembled ahead of him. At seven in the evening there was still plenty of light.

As Alexandra climbed out of the limousine, the sun gilded the white-gold strands of her hair swirled among the darker blond shades. She reminded him of an aviatrix who'd just jumped down from her biplane and pulled off her cap to reveal a riot of jaw-length curls. There was nothing artificial about her. She wore no lipstick, but with her wide, seductive mouth it wasn't necessary.

His first impression of her hadn't changed. She was totally unaware of herself. He found himself studying her naturally arched brows. They framed large, sad, luminous gray eyes set in a classically shaped face. Sometimes they were inscrutable. Other times when she talked about the debt she couldn't pay, he was shaken to the gut by their emotional intensity.

The woman he'd chosen for his bride had an innate glamour that couldn't be manufactured or purchased. He saw shocked wonder in the eyes of his pilot and staff as he introduced her. Not only was he flying back to Castelmare with his intended, but they'd just learned that Princess Alexandra Grigory was Kathryn Carlisle's daughter.

He could hear their minds making comparisons between the screen idol and her flesh-and-blood offspring. Alexandra's impenetrable gaze added a certain mystery to her demeanor that set her apart from her mother.

After a word to his pilot, Lucca joined her. Once up the steps he ushered her through the body of the plane to his study. "As soon as we're in the air, the steward will show you to your cabin where you can freshen up."

"Thank you," she whispered, not looking at him as she found a place to sit. In case she was getting cold feet, it was too late to renege on their arrangement now.

Per his instructions the pilot started the engines. Lucca noted with satisfaction that the Fasten Seat Belts sign had flashed on. The sound of her strapping herself in was music to his ears. For the first time all day he was able to let go of the tension gripping him. He fastened his.

Soon they were taxiing out to the runway. He glanced at her striking profile. She had a proud nose. He liked that. He liked everything about her. "Once we've reached altitude, I'll ask dinner to be served."

"I'm afraid I'm still full from lunch."

"Even so, you might change your mind later."

In a few minutes the engines screamed and they were moving faster. Soon the wheels left the tarmac and the jet was airborne.

Lucca felt a sense of excitement he hadn't experienced since he was a young boy taking his first ride in his father's plane, but this time it had nothing to do with power and everything to do with his passenger.

All his life he'd known the day would come when he would have to marry someone royal like himself. But to reach his midthirties and still not feel as much as a spark for one of them had thrust him into a living nightmare from which he hadn't awakened until this morning.

Who could have imagined a scenario as unlikely as the one he'd commandeered in Defore's office? Meeting Alexandra had constituted nothing short of a miracle. Their marriage would solve Sofia's problem, as well.

"Veni, vidi, vici," Lucca found himself muttering aloud. He felt like the great Roman emperor Julius Caesar who after one of his victories said, "I came, I saw, I conquered."

She glanced over at him with those hypnotic eyes. "Were you talking to me?"

It was better she didn't know what was going on in his mind. "I was telling you the seat-belt light has gone off. We've reached cruising speed. I'll ring for the steward."

By the time she'd unfastened hers, the other man appeared and requested she follow him. The second she was out the door Lucca rang one of his bodyguards and gave him a flurry of instructions he wanted followed immediately. While he waited for his bodyguard to appear, he phoned the galley and advised them to prepare some sandwiches and fruit.

In a few minutes Paolo the bodyguard entered the study, carrying a square eight-by-eight inch metallic box by the handle. Lucca took it from him and placed it on the conference table where he ate his meals.

They walked to the door and he thanked him before getting on the phone to his secretary working in the rear compartment of the jet. Bringing home a bride-to-be at the midnight hour meant dictating a ton of new instructions. When Alexandra reentered the cabin, his breath caught to realize he hadn't been hallucinating after all. She really was on the plane with him. He rang off to give her his full attention.

"Come and sit at the table. There's something I want to show you."

Her gaze fastened on the box, then swerved to his with an expression that held traces of pain. "If that's what I think it is, I don't need to see it. If I never lay eyes on another diamond again, it will be too soon."

He grimaced. "Nevertheless, you need to look at this. Every wife should know how her husband makes a living. Sit down and close your eyes."

She complied, wondering exactly what he meant. He opened the box and removed the smaller black jewel case, then lifted the lid. "You can look now."

Alex couldn't stop the gasp that escaped her throat. Nestled against silver velvet lay the teardrop-shaped diamond almost the size of an American half dollar. It was a shade of green, darker than peridot but lighter than emerald.

"The true color of nature," he spoke her thoughts.

"I didn't know a diamond could be green. The hue of the stone is utterly incredible."

He nodded his dark head. "Its color was caused by the crystals in a volcanic pipe coming into contact with a radioactive source at some point during its lifetime. The phenomenon is so rare in a diamond this size, the Ligurian is rated among the top five diamonds in the world."

"Why do you call it that?"

"Castelmare is situated on the Ligurian coast we share with Italy."

"I'm ashamed I don't know my geography better."

"Don't be. The majority of people haven't heard of it, either. In 1906 my great-grandfather started buying diamonds from the owner of a mine in South Africa, and they established a business relationship.

"As a result, he created a diamond-cutting industry in Castelmare to augment the kingdom's prosperity. Today it's a thriving concern. People from all over the world flock there to buy diamonds, which brings us a good percentage of our wealth."

"I had no idea," her voice trailed. "Forgive my temper. That's twice today." Already she was aware her soon-to-be husband soon-to-be king was a hardworking man, as well as a monarch.

With jewelry stores in New York and around the globe, this little lesson about the Ligurian diamond was just the beginning of many others. One of the most daunting would be to learn Italian. Help!

"I've already forgotten." He was a much kinder person than she was. Her Carlisle temperament had a nasty habit of coming out at precarious moments.

By agreeing to their unique marriage arrangement, she was entering a brand-new world. Only now did she realize how much she would have to learn, starting with this rare gemstone.

"It's the most exquisite thing I've ever seen."

"It's flawless from the inside out. You have no idea how rare that it is."

There was a reverence in his voice. She wondered if he was thinking about something else. Someone else...

"How many karats is it?"

A pause ensued before he said, "It is 44.16. Go ahead and hold it up so you can view the facets' reflections."

"You're not afraid I'll run off with it?"

His lips formed a half smile. "Where would you go?" he teased dryly.

The next thing she knew he reached for her right hand and placed the famous diamond in her palm much the same way he'd kissed it in the limousine. Her body had turned to jelly then, too. This had to stop! Every time he came near or touched her, she reacted the same way.

Alex couldn't believe any of today had really happened,

let alone that she was holding something this precious in her hand. When she raised it to the light, she let out another cry. "The sight's so dazzling, it hurts your eyes."

"My thoughts exactly when I saw it in its uncut state for the first time," he whispered, but he was looking down at her as he said it. She got this fluttery feeling in her chest and put the diamond back in the case.

"When was that?"

"I was on a buying trip at nineteen when the mine owner showed me what they'd just discovered. After I purchased it, I kept it hidden. A few years later I got the best diamond cutters in the business together. Between us we decided a teardrop shape would show it off to the best advantage."

"Do you keep it on display year round?"

"Except for the six weeks while I take it on a world tour doing business." He placed it in the carrying case and shut the lid. "The rest of the time it stays in a museum on the palace grounds. Several hours each day it's open to the public, where tourists can view the family jewels and various items dating from the Middle Ages."

"I can't imagine having a family history you can trace back that far."

"Have you forgotten your uncle Yuri is going to bring you your family's genealogy? He said it goes back much further."

So he did. There'd been too much information to process today. "What other kinds of business do you do?" Her curiosity had gotten the better of her.

"Banking, investments, tourism, space-age technologies."

She wanted to hear more, but the steward came in with a tray of food and drinks, interrupting them. The two men conversed in such rapid Italian that Alex despaired of ever being able to catch on, let alone speak it with any degree of fluency.

Once the steward had left them alone again, nervous-ness drove her to bite into one of the ham-and-cheese sand-wiches. Lucca sat down opposite her. What intangible force had possessed her to agree to his insane marriage proposal?

Because you felt sorry for him, a little voice inside nagged.

For once in her life she'd met someone who had an even worse problem than she did and she was in a position to help him.

Keep telling yourself that, Alex.

But what if I make a mistake? she cried inwardly, her emotions containing a hint of hysteria.

"I think you're exhausted," he commiserated, without her having said anything. It was frightening how easily he read her thoughts and moods.

She drank part of her soda. "I think I am, too. What about you?"

He'd already consumed two sandwiches and some grapes. "I still have work to do and I've never been more energized. Feel free to use my phone to call whomever you like—your boss maybe? If you'll give me the numbers, I'll make the nec-essary arrangements for your apartment and belongings."

"That's all right. I'll take care of everything tomorrow afternoon when I know I can reach people at the best time for them."

"Then why don't you go to bed. Tomorrow morning we'll be landing at seven-thirty and have breakfast on board first. Once we're ready to leave, it's a fifteen-mile hop by helicopter to the palace in Capriccio. In case you're wondering, our part of the Mediterranean is too hilly for an airport so we use our French neighbor's to the west."

"I see." Alex bit her lower lip. "Are your parents expect-ing you tomorrow?"

Over the rim of his coffee, he gave her an intense regard. *"Si."*

"Do they know about me?"

"Not yet."

She stirred restlessly. "I can't meet them looking like this."

He put the cup down. This time his brown eyes were shuttered as if his thoughts were far away. "I don't see anything wrong with the way you look."

"When I left Los Angeles I only brought one change of clothes with me. I'm afraid a casual top and trousers is hardly the kind of attire they'd expect of a future daughter-in-law."

His brows unexpectedly furrowed, giving him an almost formidable appearance. She didn't know he could look like that, and her heart skipped a beat.

"Maybe I didn't make myself clear. Ours is an unorthodox relationship."

"Oh, I'm well aware of that!" she said in a torrent of words.

"Bene," he drawled, "because nothing's going to change between you and me. What we both see is what we get. Your wardrobe from California will arrive soon enough. If you feel you need to add to it before time, then go shopping. Understood?"

Nothing could be clearer than that! Maybe one dress and some shoes to match. Beyond those items she had no more money and wouldn't ask for any.

"For the honor of the House of Savoy going back many generations, I'm doing my duty by marrying a royal," he informed her. "However, beyond the business of running the kingdom, no one, not even my parents will have the right to question either of us or dictate how we conduct our personal lives."

His final words had been delivered in code, but she'd

already deciphered it without problem: "No one, not even you, Alexandra, will have the right to question me on the way I spend my free time or how much of it will be given to the woman I love."

That was Alex's part of the pact. Naturally she intended to keep it. One of these days soon she would tell him what she was prepared to do for him and the woman he loved.

Lucca's part was to help her achieve a career that only this morning had seemed beyond the realm of possibility.

She knew he wouldn't let her down, so it defied logic why she would suddenly have this hollow feeling, almost as if she'd lost something precious even though it had never been hers in the first place.

"Thank you for the meal. I'm going to take your advice and say good-night."

He got up and followed her out the door to her cabin located midway down the lighted corridor.

She walked inside while he lingered in the doorway. Lucca was a powerful-looking male and totally gorgeous standing there in his elegant summer suit and tie. A vital, living presence even though he must have been up with the birds. Alex knew she wasn't in a dream, but it felt like it.

"Are you comfortable in here?"

His deep voice permeated to her insides. Why on earth was she feeling shy? "The steward has seen to everything. Thank you."

"Is there anything else you need *I* can do for you?"

She rubbed her upper arms with her hands for want of something to do with them. "After uniting me with my great-uncle and making it possible for me to go to medical school—that is, if I make it in—I'd be an ungrateful wretch to ask you for anything else."

"Ungrateful wretch?" He did an exaggerated imitation, making her laugh once more. "Your language has its colorful moments. Life with you is going to be…fascinating." Maybe it was a trick of light, but she thought he looked pleased. "Now I'll teach you your second word in Italian. *Buonanotte,* Alexandra."

"Buonanotte."

"Lucca," came the reminder.

"Lucca."

He gave a nod of approbation. "You have an excellent ear. The best kind of omen for the future." So saying, he quietly closed the door.

Alex's feet stayed rooted in place.

The Prince of Castelmare was happy——possibly happier than he'd ever been in his life because he'd solved his problem.

Of course he was still wide-awake! Now that Alex had gone to bed he could phone his lover and tell her a miracle had happened. He'd found his way out of the abyss that had been burying him alive all these years.

Yet just imagining the other woman's joy sent a surprising stab of pain through Alex's heart, causing her to stagger for a moment.

CHAPTER FOUR

"Lucca?" His sister's anxious cry almost broke his eardrum.

It was the middle of the night, yet she sounded as if she hadn't been to bed yet. Not so the members of the palace staff he could trust. They'd already received a rude awakening from his nocturnal phone calls. At the moment they were busy carrying out his orders.

"*Ciao*, Regina."

"Please don't tell me you're not coming home. It's been close to two months. I've run all the interference with the parents I can."

"No man ever had a better friend. Only one more favor."

"Lucca—"

"*Scusimi, cara.* Don't talk, just listen. This is important." He heard a groan.

"It's four-thirty palace time. In three hours the helicopter will be waiting to fly you to the airport in Nice. We need privacy, so we'll meet for breakfast on board the jet."

"But—"

"No questions now. I've been working half the night and need a few hours' sleep before the plane lands. All will be answered when we see each other. *Ciao*."

Lucca clicked off. Now that everything had been set in motion, he could pass out. After putting his phone on the bedside table, he turned on his stomach and buried his face in the pillow for what was left of the night.

"Your Highness?"

Through waves of torpor he heard the steward's voice and let out a moan.

"*Si*. What is it?"

"You asked me to waken you at seven."

Lucca frowned before glancing at his watch. He'd been asleep three hours already? How was that possible?

"Is Princess Alexandra up yet?"

"If she is, she hasn't left her cabin."

The thought of seeing her this morning produced an adrenaline rush, bringing him fully awake. "Before we're ready to land, ask her to join me in the study."

He nodded and left the cabin.

Once Lucca had showered and shaved, he opened his closet doors. After a quick perusal, "The tan suit I think with the brown silk shirt. No tie," he muttered to himself.

Five minutes later he entered the study to discover she was seated near the window drinking coffee. Filled with relief that yesterday's earthshaking events hadn't been a figment of his imagination, his muscles relaxed.

"*Buongiorno, Alexandra.*"

"*Buongiorno, Lucca. Come va?*"

She must have asked the steward for help. It pleased him she was already trying to communicate in his native tongue. One day she would be fluent.

"*Va bene. Grazie.*" His gaze took in her plum-colored silk mandarin-collar shirt and gray denims. She had superb dress sense. Most Italian women of his personal acquaintance weren't as tall. None had her artless sophistication. When he realized he was staring, he poured himself coffee from the tray placed on the table. Then he sat down opposite her. "How did you sleep?"

She smoothed some hair away from her temple in an unconsciously feminine gesture. "Probably as well as you did."

He chuckled before swallowing the hot liquid. "If we're always this honest with each other, we'll have no problems."

"Lucca—" She put her mug in the drink holder. "This is all new territory for both of us and we'll have to make it up as we go along, but there are a few things we need to discuss before I meet your parents." Her breathlessness was more pronounced this morning, a sign her composure was only surface deep.

"You took the words out of my mouth. As soon as we land, I'll do my best to prepare you so you'll feel at ease."

In reaction to his comment she rolled those fabulous eyes of hers. The unexpected gesture made him smile. Along with everything else about her, Alexandra had a healthy sense of humor. Living with her was going to be fun.

With perfect timing the seat-belt light flashed on. "Have you been to Europe before?"

"No."

They both buckled up.

"I envy you seeing everything for the first time."

Her knuckles looked white where she gripped the armrests. "If there is a first time."

Lucca's laughter resounded in the cabin. He'd done this hundreds of times before, but had forgotten the steep descent wasn't to everyone's taste. While she took in the view of one of the world's most famous coastlines, he preferred to concentrate on the view seated across from him. She was all soft shoulders and long legs.

Mio dio, her mouth…

* * *

No sooner had they taxied to a stop than Lucca was at his desk, talking to someone on the phone. Alex sensed a hum of activity both in and outside the plane.

Cocooned as she was in the body of the jet, she felt a certain comfort in being relatively isolated from the world, but her heart did a double clutch to realize that before long she'd be stepping into his world. The gravity of what she'd done was starting to seep in.

Footsteps in the corridor drew her attention away from the window where she could see men and maintenance vehicles clustering around to service the plane. Her ear picked up a woman's voice.

Alex felt her stomach muscles bunch in apprehension. Lucca had virtually promised her they'd talk before she met his parents. Surprised she might not be able to trust him after all, she turned to him. However, no words escaped because the steward had just wheeled in a cart of food. Behind him came a woman who couldn't possibly be his mother.

"Lucca—" cried the adorable-looking female who launched herself at him. She was maybe five-four with a cap of glossy black curls and a figure to rival that of Gina Lollobrigida.

Alex's boss, Michelle, had worked around movie stars for years and thought the curvaceous Italian film idol of the fifties was the essence of feminine beauty. Apparently, Lucca thought the same thing. Was this the woman he loved? His dark eyes flashed with emotion as he rushed around to crush her in his arms.

"Regina," he murmured.

The sight of him rocking her curvy body dressed in a trendy-looking, ribbed top in navy with white cargo pants drew a groan from Alex. Though she'd made a promise to herself to help the two of them all she could, she hadn't expected to be thrown in at the deep end this fast.

Obviously, something very private was going on. The other woman was crying gut-wrenching tears. They seemed to pour from her soul, and why not? After all, the separation must be brutal for both of them. Even Alex with only ten Italian words in her vocabulary at the moment could tell he was crooning endearments to her. Suddenly she knew a terrible envy to be loved like that.

The steward continued to lay out breakfast, seemingly oblivious to their uninhibited reunion. Alex wished she could remain as unaffected. Shocked by another strange jolt of pain and embarrassed for anyone to notice, she turned her head away and ended up looking blindly out the window again.

"Regina? I want you to meet someone." Lucca had switched to English. That was Alex's cue to give them her attention. With pounding heart, she pivoted around, then came to an abrupt stop because the lovely face and moist eyes staring at her was the feminine version of Lucca's.

She was his sister!

A wave of intense relief washed over Alex, catching her by surprise. She clung to the back of the seat.

"May I present Princess Alexandra Carlisle Grigory of Beverly Hills, California. Alexandra? I would like you to meet my one and only sibling, Princess Regina Schiaparelli Vittorio."

"How do you do?" both women said at once and shook hands. The puzzled, curious look in his sister's expression couldn't hope to match Alex's dazed condition. In trying to recover, she made the mistake of glancing at Lucca.

His eyes were so alive Alex knew he had to be thinking about the freedom he now had. It wouldn't be long now before he could go to his lover and tell her there was a way they could be together. "Regina, I wanted you to be the first to know that Alexandra has consented to be my wife."

Following that revelation a gasp broke from his sister. Her eyes, a burgundy brown, stared at Alex in shock before darting to Lucca. "I-is this the truth?" she stammered, as if she were afraid to believe it.

"As God is my witness," came his solemn response.

Alex wasn't prepared for the way Regina's eyes lit up or her strong hug that came close to knocking Alex down. It was a good thing she was taller and could take the impact.

Once again Lucca's sister was sobbing, but these seemed to be happy sobs for her brother who appeared to have picked the bride he wanted. All these years Regina had to have been aware of Lucca's pain. Now she was misinterpreting the situation, but it didn't matter. In witnessing the degree of love Regina felt for her brother, Alex was more determined than ever to facilitate matters for the two lovers.

Already Alex loved Regina for being so devoted to him. This was the way family should be, all for one and one for all. Lucca's happiness was the goal that would bind her friendship with his sister.

Over Regina's heaving shoulder, Alex met Lucca's gaze. His dark orbs were thanking her. She smiled slowly at him, letting him know he could trust her to be his friend. He smiled back. The moment was so piercingly sweet she closed her eyes to savor it.

In the next instant Regina moved out of his arms. "Forgive me," she said, wiping her eyes. "What a beginning!"

"Being an only child I've always wondered what it would be like to have a sister," Alex confided. "I'm no longer nervous."

Regina laughed gently, but was still shaking her head, bewildered. "How did it happen? Where did you two meet? When? Mama and Papa know nothing! This has to be the best-kept secret of the century."

Better stick to the truth as much as possible. "In a round-about way through my mother."

"That's right. On business," Lucca added. "Let's eat while we talk, shall we?" By tacit agreement the three of them sat down at the table.

Breakfast for a king, that's what had been ordered. Alex was starving. She filled her plate with a little bit of every-thing and ate her fill. Lucca's healthy appetite told its own story this morning, but Regina was too excited to eat more than a peach.

"Men are never good with the details, so I want to hear the whole thing from you, Alexandra."

Alex flashed Lucca a signal of distress but he was no help and bit into another roll with those beautiful white teeth of his. Apparently he and his sister had few secrets…except the biggest one.

"My mother died a little more than five months ago leaving a large debt. Her attorney advised me to sell her diamonds and suggested the House of Savoy in New York. I flew out and—"

"And that's how we met," Lucca took over. "The attrac-tion between us caught us both by surprise. It will interest you to know that Alexandra's mother was Kathryn Carlisle, the film star. Her first husband was Alexandra's father, Prince Oleg Grigory."

Regina cocked her head and studied Alex for a full min-ute. "With those Russian roots, I think you're even more beautiful than your mother and that's saying a lot considering I've seen several of her pictures. Trust my brother to find the cream over in America."

She breathed deeply. "Thank you, Regina. I feel the same way about him. We complement each other in the ways that are most important." What else could she say? Theirs wasn't a love match or anything close to it, but Lucca expected her to reciprocate his affection in front of the public and his family. That's what he'd said.

"With many discoveries still to be made," Lucca imparted unexpectedly. His hand closed over hers across the table. "Isn't that right, *bellissima?*"

A glorious word to hear from a man *if* he truly loved you.

Alex crinkled her nose. "That's what has me worried, Regina. I sing off-key, I'm messy and I don't know if I snore. There, Lucca." She squeezed his hand before letting it go. Hers was on fire. "That's my confession for today. Tomorrow, three more."

Lucca threw his head back and laughed. Regina joined him. When it subsided she said, "I could tell you a lot of things about my brother."

"But you won't," he clipped out. "Let Alexandra discover them one at a time so I don't scare her off."

"Is there a reason why she's not wearing the betrothal ring yet?"

"*Si, piccina.* All the reason in the world. I didn't happen to be carrying it around with me when I left on business weeks ago."

"Besides, Lucca knows I don't like rings," Alex inserted before he could say anything else. "In between working toward my degree, I've been a makeup artist at a movie studio for the past eight years. Rings and bracelets just get in the way."

"Even so," he supplied, "we've decided on a simple gold wedding band at the ceremony. That's all two people need to symbolize their true feelings."

"I agree," Regina murmured as if she had something else on her mind. "What did you major in?"

"Biology."

"You've led an amazing life."

Alex's gaze collided with Lucca's before she looked away. "I was rather thinking the same thing about you, Regina. My father died before I was a year old, and I was raised by nannies. I didn't grow up in a palace like Castelmare with two doting parents and grandparents and a loving brother like Lucca."

"Which brings us to the subject at hand," he stated in a way Alex was coming to recognize as his monarch voice. He'd used it at the store when she'd tried to get away from him. "Alexandra will be living at the palace from now on. Until the ceremony I've arranged for her to sleep in the blue suite next to yours, Regina."

"I hoped you'd suggest it. I'd love it if Alexandra were close to me. It's lonely down that hall."

"I thought you might like the idea." Lucca grinned. "She's eager to learn Italian, and I can't think of a better way for her to pick it up than to spend time with you after her lessons."

"I'll ring Professor Emilio. He'll be the best teacher for her, Lucca. Between sightseeing and shopping, it won't be long before she's rattling off Italian with me."

"*Bene.* I knew I could count on you." He sounded inordinately pleased with his sister's ideas.

Alex smiled at her, reassured by her warmth and generous nature. "You and Lucca speak impeccable English. I'm very impressed."

"Thank you. We had excellent teachers and spent time in England."

"It shows. How many languages do you speak?"

"Five."

"Now *that's* incredible."

"Not really. Papa speaks a dozen." Regina's expression suddenly grew sober. "Has Lucca told you how sick he's been?"

"Yes. I'm so sorry."

"When he hears the news about you two, he'll be overjoyed. Mama and I are convinced it will add years to his life."

"Knowing Lucca is going to take over will come as a major release for him, I'm certain of it," Alex assured her.

On that note her husband-to-be got up from the table and came around to place his hands on her shoulders, massaging them gently. "What do you say we fly on to the palace. I'm anxious to get you installed and comfortable. This evening will be soon enough to present you to our parents."

Her relief was so great that he was going to give her the rest of the day to get her bearings that she wasn't prepared when he leaned over without warning and kissed the side of her neck. Regina was getting the totally wrong impression of the way things really were, but that was the whole idea.

The feel of his mouth against her hot skin was positively erotic. Liquid fire ran its course through her body. She wasn't sure she could leave the cabin on her own power. Her weakness increased when Lucca put his hand behind her neck and guided her out of the jet into a lovely warm June midmorning.

They walked a short distance to the waiting helicopter.

Regina and her own bodyguards had gone ahead of them. Lucca's bodyguards stayed close. Paolo was the last one inside the ten-passenger interior before they lifted off.

Alex didn't know why, but all of a sudden the upward movement seemed to break the trance she'd been in for the past twenty-four hours. The people surrounding her were strangers, all speaking a language she didn't understand.

The sight of the gleaming white jet with its royal coat of arms receding from view was as unfamiliar as the curved coastline bordering the plain of Nice. She was being whisked away to the home of the future king of Castelmare. In four weeks, she would be his wife.

Like a leaf tossed in the wind, she was rootless, being swept along over high-perched villages and blue-green water by some unseen force so much greater than she could comprehend, she started to shiver and couldn't stop.

A hard-muscled arm slid around her shoulders. Lucca pulled her into his side as close as the straps would allow. "It'll be all right," he whispered into her hair. "You should have told me you don't like helicopters. We could have driven the short distance instead. Just cling to me. We'll be landing on the north grounds of the palace in two minutes. I swear it."

"I'm fine," she croaked, too shaken by events to correct his erroneous assumption. He smelled divinely male and felt so solid she rested against him, needing his strength. She was probably creasing the expensive-looking tan suit adorning his striking male physique, but he didn't seem to mind.

By the time they landed on the helipad, her tremors had subsided. To her chagrin other sensations had taken over she didn't want to feel or acknowledge. Fearing he could sense her emotional turmoil, she undid her seat belt and stood up, forcing him to relinquish his hold on her. At the same time she noticed the speculative glance Regina had given her and Lucca.

One day Regina would observe too closely and learn the truth, that she and Lucca were only playacting. Though her brother was in love with another woman, he had to walk a fine line in order to convince everyone his marriage to Alex was built on solid ground. For the moment she had to respond like a woman in love, yet already she was worn-out with the strain of it and longed to be alone to think.

When it came her turn to climb out of the helicopter with Lucca's assistance, she noticed a swarm of staff from the palace descending on them. The crown prince and favorite son had come home at last.

No sooner did that thought fill her mind than Regina put a hand on Alex's arm. "Now that we've arrived, my brother's life won't be his own. Come on. I'll show you to your suite. After a transatlantic flight I'm always exhausted, even if I've slept." Regina understood a great deal.

Lucca stood behind her and gave her waist a surreptitious squeeze, melting her insides. "Go with my sister," he whispered before kissing her temple. "I'll ring you later in the day when you've had a chance to rest." It was clear there'd be no introductions to anyone until she'd been presented to his parents.

Alex nodded without looking at him and followed Regina's lead, but with each stride that took her away from him, she felt the keen loss of his presence.

Better get used to it, Alex. Lucca is only a figurehead in your life. Concentrate on obtaining your goals, then you won't be a pathetic creature who listens for his every foot-

step and hangs like a heavy millstone around his neck.
Focus on your surroundings.

Her surroundings…

She paused midway to the north portico at the rear of
the sprawling Renaissance palace. It was perched on the
lower part of a steep hillside. In the late-morning sun the
ornate, three-story structure gleamed like a dazzling white
jewel against a backdrop of an impossibly blue sea and sky.

Her gaze lifted to the stunning flag with a white cross
on a red field designating the House of Savoy. Below it was
a flag with a crown and shield of the reigning Vittorio
family coat-of-arms. She'd seen the same insignia embla-
zoned on the jet's exterior.

Everywhere her eyes traveled she discovered fruit and
palm trees. Flower gardens with too many varieties to name
dotted the fluid carpet of velvety green. The marvelous
scent of roses mixed with lemon and orange filled her lungs.

Southern California had its share of fabulous estates, but
nothing she'd ever seen came close to this. Regina walked
back to her. "It's breathtaking to me, too, and I've lived here
all my life."

"No ordinary gardener created this paradise. It's been
done by a master planner. I'm staggered by so much beauty."

Regina's heart-shaped mouth curved into a smile that lit
her warm brown eyes. "I'll tell Dizo what you said."

"Who's that?"

"His real name is Dinozzo. He's the oldest son of Guido
Fornese, the head gardener, but between you and me Dizo
is the genius. I'd never say that to anyone else because I
wouldn't want to hurt Guido's feelings."

"I'll never tell," Alex assured her.

The younger woman stared at her. "You're nice."

"So are you, Regina." She had a sweetness in her. Though they were only a year apart in age, their life's experience had been so different Alex felt much older.

"Wait till you see the view of the front from your bedroom balcony."

Alex put a hand to her breast. "Do you think my heart can take it?" she teased to cover her emotions spilling all over the place.

In that lovely face raised to her she saw traces of the charismatic man who'd cast a spell over her. Otherwise why would she be standing in this Garden of Eden instead of a cubicle on the studio lot in Culver City building a nose for Cyrano de Bergerac.

Gentle laughter broke from Regina. "I'm still alive if that means anything."

"It means a lot."

"There's another reason why Lucca wants you in the blue suite."

"What is that?" Alex asked quietly.

"I'd better not tell. You'll find out soon enough." The comment made her feel giddy with curiosity. "Come on, before he gets after me for not taking the proper care of you."

The palace had a staff of a small army of people, two of whom opened the doors for her and Regina. Alex stepped onto a checkerboard floor of deep rose and white marble. Across the grand foyer rose an exquisitely carved marble staircase. The walls and niches were filled with statuary and gold-framed paintings of immense size.

When Regina noticed Alex's interest in everything, she said, "The core of the present palazzo dates from 1467 and was originally the town residence of an ambitious Capriccio banker. The ruling family of the House of Savoy liked the location and bought it in 1498. The families that came after began to build on to it, filling it with great treasures until it looks the way it does today."

"You're surrounded by history," Alex marveled. "The palace is absolutely beautiful inside and out."

"I think so, too. Some of the most precious items have been moved to the museum so visitors can see them." They started up the stairs to the second floor.

"Lucca told me the family jewels are kept there."

"Yes, including the Ligurian diamond. Did you happen to see it on display in New York?"

"Only a glimpse, but during the flight here he let me hold it up to the light so I could see into its heart," she explained as they curved around to the next story.

Regina paused on the top step to study her for a moment. Alex had no way of deciphering the other woman's thoughts before following her down the spacious corridor. Everywhere she looked the ceilings and walls were a masterpiece of frescoes and gilt cornices forming frames around them.

When Regina opened the double doors halfway down the east wing, Alex let out a cry of delight. The large apartment with its ornate white woodwork was a vision of blue and white stripes against a smaller blue-and-white pattern on the walls.

Through one set of double doors was a den with a computer and every possible accoutrement for her comfort.

"Lucca will have ordered a lunch tray for you. He wants you to relax and enjoy yourself."

"Thank you for everything, Regina."

"You're welcome. If you need anything, pick up the phone and dial 1 for housekeeping. Dial 2 for Lucca, 3 for me and 0 for an outside line. Talk to you later."

Dial 2 for Lucca…

Regina shut the doors behind her, leaving Alex, who was charmed by her new world. A fabulous blue-and-white Persian rug covered the gleaming white, marble floors of the sitting room. She walked across it to the bedroom. Alex saw that her suitcase had already been placed at the end of the king-size bed. At the opposite end of the room was a fireplace framed by hand-painted blue-and-white tiles. Exquisite.

Tall French doors had been opened to reveal Capriccio's curved bay with its myriad of yachts. Drawn to the balcony, she looked down on the terraced grounds where she saw a long, blue rectangular pool graced by ornamental flowering trees and statuary. Exotic plants delineated the borders of each terrace. Steps led down to the private beach. Between the view and the warm, sweetly scented air, the whole ambience was out of a dream and left her speechless.

"After your fright on the helicopter, I didn't think you'd make it any further than the bed."

Lucca's deep male voice jarred her out of her trance. She turned around but couldn't see him.

"Look up."

Surprised, she lifted her head and discovered him staring down at her from a balcony on the third floor, one suite over.

"I put you in there so I could keep an eye on you without an audience."

She assumed he meant the bodyguards. Minus his suit jacket, he was leaning on his forearms, giving her the impression he'd been out there for several minutes and was happy to be home after being away so long. Knowing there were no secrets between the two of them had to make this the supreme moment of his life.

Alex wished she could feel happier about it. "I thought you'd be with your parents."

"I spoke to them from the plane. They're expecting me at five this evening after Papa's nap."

"So they still don't know about me?"

"No. I'll come for you at ten to five. We'll make our entrance together. In the meantime I have business I must attend to. Enjoy your meal. It happens to be one of my favorites."

Alex couldn't fault him for anything.

As he turned away, she glimpsed the play of muscle in those masculine shoulders covered by his silk shirt. His well-honed physique was proof he kept fit. Not wanting to think where his personal business might take him this afternoon, she went back inside the apartment to eat. One of the maids had set the tray on the oval table in the sitting room.

Though the scallops and pasta were delicious, she ate with little enthusiasm, leaving most of it to start making phone calls home. Michelle was her first priority. Alex glanced at her watch. Her boss would be up and getting ready for work by now. Once she arrived on the lot, pure chaos reigned. Now would be the best time to catch her.

Alex hadn't been looking forward to telling her she wouldn't be coming back to work. For the moment all she would say was that while she was in New York, she realized she needed a complete break from her life in California. For the time being she was looking into attending medical school and would get in touch with her when her plans solidified.

As for her apartment, she would phone her landlord and arrange through him to get her belongings packed and shipped to Castelmare. Her used car could be dealt with through the car dealership where she'd purchased it.

Her last call would be to Mr. Watkins who'd be shocked about the faux diamonds. For the moment, all he needed to know was that she wouldn't be returning to California for a while.

Later on she would tell him the truth. He alone would understand why she was ready to do anything to pay off her mother's debt, even to being a stand-in consort for an equally desperate prince. But kind as Mr. Watkins was, he wouldn't fail to remind her that two wrongs still made a wrong.

Deep in her psyche Alex knew what she was doing was wrong, but it was far too late to back out now. She was more her mother's daughter than she wanted to admit.

CHAPTER FIVE

AT QUARTER to five Alex stood in front of the bathroom mirror wearing the newly cleaned and pressed outfit she'd worn to the jewelry store yesterday. The maid who'd taken her lunch tray away had seen to it. Naturally it had to have been on Lucca's suggestion since he knew Alex only had two outfits with her.

She brushed her freshly washed hair into some semblance of order. It would cooperate for all of five minutes, then the natural curl would take on a life of its own and become unruly once more. In deference to meeting his parents, she applied a soft pink lipstick.

Since talking with her boss and Mr. Watkins, both of whom had been surprisingly understanding and supportive of her plans, she'd tried to sleep, but it never came. No matter how much she rationalized it, her conscience wouldn't allow her to forget she and Lucca were about to perpetrate a great fraud on his family.

When she heard a knock on the door of the suite, she jumped. Her nerves were frayed to the point she wanted to hide.

"Alexandra? I'm coming in." The next thing she knew

Lucca was striding over the threshold, his hard-muscled legs covered in casual stone-colored trousers.

Her stunned gaze lifted to the navy cotton crew-neck pullover stretched across his powerful frame with the sleeves pushed up to the elbows. With his black wavy hair and striking aquiline features, his looks transcended every known superlative in her vocabulary.

He'd purposely worn an outfit that would make her comfortable in hers. Everything he did was for her welfare, causing her to care a little more for him when she didn't want to.

They met halfway across the sitting room. To her dismay she was out of breath. His dark eyes searched hers with an intensity that made it impossible to look away. "Only one thing is missing. Stand still while I pin this on you."

He reached in his trouser pocket and pulled something out. She assumed it was a family heirloom of some kind, but almost fainted when she glimpsed the unmistakable Ligurian diamond suspended beneath a small gold crown. In one deft move he'd attached it to the draped part of her blouse covering her right shoulder.

How could he have had the jewel fashioned into a pin this fast?

She pressed her hand against it, as shaken by the brush of his fingers against her skin through the thin material as anything else. "What have you done?" she cried in panic. "I can't wear *this!*"

"Why not?" came his mellow query. "It's mine to give and was meant to be worn by a woman of your height and looks. No one else could carry it off."

Heat scorched her cheeks. "I'm not my mother!"

"That's true. You're your own self with a little of her thrown in."

"You know what I meant. This is a mockery."

"Only in your mind."

She tried to remove it, but Lucca prevented it, shaking his dark head with a determination that sent shivers down her spine. "This is my signature. The sight of it will convince my father I'm happy with my choice of bride and am ready at last to relieve him of his burdens."

He had an answer for everything. It stopped her every time. "You should have given this to the woman you love." Her voice trembled. "She alone has the right."

Lucca gave an unconscious shrug of his broad shoulders. "You're going to be my wife. It's expected that you wear a family jewel. Nothing in the museum would suit you better than this. Are you ready?"

No, she wanted to scream, but she didn't dare. On the ride to the airport a century ago she'd agreed to marry him and she had no right to question what he felt was necessary to make his parents happy.

After reaching for her purse, she followed him to the door of her suite. As she moved past him their bodies touched. She might as well have come in contact with a current of electricity and rushed into the hall ahead of him.

Carlo stood a short distance away. He probably saw her reaction. Great. Lucca never went anywhere without him. His permanent shadow. The bodyguard probably pitied Alex who was going to be nothing more than a token wife. Alex didn't want his pity. The thought sickened her.

"Is everything all right?" Lucca asked with concern. "My parents are waiting for me in the sitting room of their apartment, but if you need more time…"

Me, he'd said. Not *us.* She shuddered.

She flashed him a little smile. "Not time, just courage."

"I promise you they're wonderful people."

"They would have to be in order to raise a man like you…and Regina," she added as an afterthought so he wouldn't get the wrong idea. Already she was letting things slip he could misinterpret.

"She likes you, Alexandra, not simply for my sake." When Alex shook her head he said, "Believe it or not, that's what she told me a little while ago. My sister's a good judge of character. I'm glad you're going to get along."

If he was glad, she was, too. He dictated their pace down the hall toward the west end. He had to know she'd never been this nervous in her life. Though he pointed out various murals from his family history in an effort to put her at ease, she wasn't in a mood to appreciate his anecdotes, amusing as they were.

They could have been out for a leisurely stroll on the palace grounds instead of inside its walls walking the plank. That's what it felt like to Alex.

When they neared the double doors where more palace personnel were on guard, Lucca reached for her hand. His hooded eyes flicked to hers. "Your presence is going to add a year, maybe even several to my father's life. For that you have my undying gratitude." With another disturbing kiss to her palm, he opened both doors.

By tacit agreement they moved inside the sumptuously decorated room, yet it showed signs of modernization with several comfortable-looking couches and chairs with ottomans. Lucca left her side long enough to kiss his parents, who were casually dressed in pants and shirts. Both sat in front of a television set.

While they conversed in Italian, she hung back where she could study his attractive mother. She was small-framed with stylishly short dark hair, an older version of Regina both in coloring and features. Alex sobered, however, at the sight of his thin father, who shut off the TV with the remote. It sounded as if they'd been watching a golf match.

No doubt the recent loss of weight and hair was due to his chemo treatments, but she could tell he'd been a very handsome man when he'd been healthy, just like his son. An oxygen tank with tubes rested against the side of his chair. This was a sight the public would never be allowed to see. The significance of it weighed on her.

Lucca stood up and turned to her, motioning her forward. In English he said, "Mama? Papa? I brought someone home from America with me. Please speak in English until she learns our language."

"Don't get up," Alex begged when they both started to rise.

His mother's brown eyes caught sight of the diamond pin, and she let out a surprised cry. "Look, Rudy!"

"I see it, Betta," her husband's voice shook. He sounded shocked and upset. "What does this mean, *figlio mio?*"

In a lightning move Lucca reached for Alex and put his arm around her waist, drawing her breathtakingly close to his side. "It means there's going to be a wedding." He smiled down at her, kissing the side of her cheek. "Who knew my gorgeous bride-to-be has been waiting in the States all this time for me to find her. If I'd known about her sooner, we would have been married ages ago and would probably have had a child or two by now."

Oh, please don't make the lie any worse than it is, Lucca.

"May I introduce you to your future daughter-in-law, Princess Alexandra Carlisle Grigory."

"Grigory?" His father's hazel eyes rounded. By now he'd gotten to his feet with some difficulty. Now she knew where Lucca's height had come from. His wife joined him. Both were nonplussed.

"Alexandra, these are my parents Rudolfo and Isabetta."

"It's wonderful to meet you at last," Alex whispered shakily. Lucca held on to her and hugged her tighter. "Her mother was the American film star Kathryn Carlisle, who tragically passed away this last Christmas Day. Her father, Prince Oleg, died when she was only nine months old. She never knew her grandfather, Prince Nicholas. However, her great-uncle Yuri is still alive and will be giving her away.

"The three of us spent a very enjoyable afternoon together at the Russian Federation in New York while he helped Alexandra become better acquainted with her Grigory heritage. He'll be sending you and Mama formal greetings right away."

His mother's brown eyes brimmed with tears before she hurried around the low table to clap her hands on Lucca's cheeks. "You've made me the happiest mother in the world," she said in English before switching to Italian. The muttered endearments needed no translation. After hugging him hard, she turned to embrace Alex.

"Welcome to the family, Alexandra. Except for when the children were born, this is the most joyful day of our married lives."

"It certainly is," Lucca's father concurred, and leaned closer to kiss Alex on both cheeks. She could detect his shallow breathing. "However, I know half a dozen young women who'll want to scratch your eyes out, as my little Regina would say."

"Rudy," his wife scolded him with mock feeling. "Lucca's made his choice. Let that be the end of it."

Lucca caught Alex from behind and pulled her against his chest where she could feel the strong solid beat of his heart. "The truth is, from the moment she and I met in New York, it was love at first sight for both of us."

Alex swallowed a groan. How gallantly he played the part when he knew his parents were aware he'd chosen her out of duty. But being nobles themselves, they would pretend this was a love match and treat her accordingly. Only one person would be able to intervene for Lucca's personal happiness. That would be his arranged wife, Alex.

His father's eyes flicked from the diamond to his son's face. He nodded solemnly. "I can tell. There's a light in your eyes that was never there before."

The king's playacting was beyond comprehension.

"I see it, too, Rudy. Have you told your sister?"

"*Si, Mama.*"

All three of them should be given the Oscar that had always eluded Alex's mother.

Lucca let go of Alex long enough to help his father be seated once more, then he pulled Alex down next to him on the opposite couch and grasped her hand in a gesture of ownership his parents couldn't fail to notice. "They met this morning after the plane landed in Nice. Alexandra will be staying in the blue suite next to Regina's until our wedding."

"That's as it should be," his mother emoted. "Now we'll all have time to get acquainted before the ceremony."

"Regina's wonderful," Alex interjected, knowing something was expected of her. In this case she'd told the truth. Lucca's sister had the same charisma as her brother. Already Alex liked them all too much.

Lucca's thumb started making lazy circles against her palm, sending sensations like shooting stars through her veins. "Alexandra is everything I could ever want. With her at my side, I look forward to taking over from you, Papa. In fact, I wish the wedding could be moved up a week. Not only for your sake, but for mine," his voice ended on a husky inflection. The next thing Alex knew he'd brushed his lips against hers.

Ohh.

His father cleared his throat. "What do you think, Betta?"

"You're still the king. It's for you to say. Why not?"

He slapped his hand against his knee. "Then so be it. A little Russian blood in our grandchildren will be an exciting addition." Help! "You want children?" His father eyed Alex frankly.

Since she knew it wouldn't happen, she said, "Of course. Having been an only child I'd love three or four."

The king's face lit up. "That settles it. We'll have a wedding here in three weeks." His wife nodded in obvious delight.

"*Grazie, Papa.*" Lucca stated as his hand slid up Alex's back and around her shoulders. "Because we can't wait any longer."

"He always was in a hurry," his father confided to Alex. "If I'm going to hold one of them on my lap before the end, that's probably a good thing."

"You'll hold more than one, Papa!" his son vowed, forgetting that theirs was a marriage in name only, but Alex understood that he'd blurted the declaration out of fear over his father's fragile state of health.

"Yuri gave Alexandra an envelope with Grigory family memorabilia. I've been working with my secretary on it since we arrived. He's already delivered a list to yours so the invitations can be finished and sent out immediately."

If that was true, then Lucca hadn't had an opportunity to see his lover yet.

To Alex's surprise he rose to his feet and drew her with him. As they started to leave, his father called out, "Wait...we've barely visited yet. Where are you going?" The longing in his voice was a beautiful thing to witness. Lucca had a father's love. Alex envied him that.

"Out," Lucca said in that commanding voice. "After this news you need to rest while Mama and Regina get the ball rolling."

"He's right, Rudy," his mother said, patting her husband's arm.

"There are things I want to show my bride-to-be, but we'll be back," Lucca said from the double doors. "I'm home to stay, Papa. Every day until the wedding you and I will spend a little time going over your affairs. I'll never be able to fill your shoes, but when the time comes, I promise to be ready to take on your cares."

Alex felt his avowal to the depths of her soul. Before he shut the doors behind them, she saw his father weep against his wife's shoulder.

Outside in the hall Lucca turned to her, grasping both her hands. His dark eyes traveled over her features with such intensity she was witless. "How do I thank you for what you did in there? They love you already." He kissed her fingertips.

She'd said too much, but she'd had no choice. "I was never given the opportunity to do anything for my parents, but I felt your parents' happiness, Lucca. This is the next best thing." Alex cleared her throat. "Besides, I haven't forgotten the pact we made. With your help I'm going after a career that will pay off all my debts including the one to you. So you don't need to thank me for anything."

His chest rose and fell with visible emotion. Not wanting to prolong the moment, for fear he could see into the deepest corners of her psyche, she said, "And now if you don't mind, I'd like to take a walk around Capriccio before dark by myself. I'm in the mood to explore. Is that permitted?"

Though his facial expression didn't change, she felt a stillness steal through him. Slowly he released her hands. "Of course. You've been assigned bodyguards, but they'll be unobtrusive. Always come and go through the north doors of the palace. Follow the road out to the west gate."

"I'll remember."

After another sweep of his eyes he said, "Do you have enough money in case you need to buy something?"

"Yes."

The fact that he didn't put up an argument or insist that they be together on their first night in Castelmare underlined the depth of his eagerness to be somewhere else, with someone else. She wasn't about to deny him that joy. The sooner she and Lucca began leading their separate lives the way it had been decided on the plane, the better. To accept the status quo with grace would be her motto starting now.

He stayed with her until they reached the grand staircase. "Have a pleasant evening, Alexandra."

Suddenly there was an aloofness emanating from him. It was a feeling foreign to her. "Thank you, Your Highness. I'd better get used to saying it."

Lines marred his arresting features. "You've never called me that before. Please never do it again."

She blinked. "I'm sorry. I meant n—"

"My name is Lucca," he broke in on a terse note. "Except for our wedding day where you'll have to address me as Your Majesty when you pledge your loyalty to your sovereign king and husband, I never want to hear anything else. *Capisci?*"

Her heart slammed against her ribs. She understood that word well enough. Alex had angered him. *"Capisci."*

"Lucca," he corrected her.

Alex repeated the words aloud, then continued on to her bedroom. With every step she felt his piercing gaze on her retreating back. He really disliked being reminded he was royalty. In retrospect she realized it came from years of knowing he would have to put his personal happiness aside to follow in his father's footsteps.

But now that had all changed for him. By getting engaged to Alex, he'd become a free man. Ironically it now appeared *she* was the one in bondage. Her hand moved instinctively to the diamond pin. Before she went anywhere else, she needed to take it off.

The loss of her mother's real diamonds hadn't been Alex's fault, but heaven help her if something happened to Lucca's prized possession. On the plane she'd sensed it had a significance for him beyond its monetary value.

Once she'd removed it she felt better. After putting it away she reached for her purse and left the suite. She was glad she didn't bump into Regina. His sister would ask questions. Alex dreaded having to explain why she and Lucca weren't together on his first night home.

At the outer gate where the palace grounds met the coastal road she could tell her bodyguards had formed a network around her. You wouldn't know them for the

Castelmarians walking up and down the street. Until she and Lucca divorced and went their separate ways, they would always be with her. It was another thing she had to get used to.

She soon discovered that the palace and grounds bordering the Mediterranean were positioned like the center jewel in Capriccio's crown. The capitol city itself was sprawled on either side and above. The steep roads zigzagged to dizzying heights where she saw the crowns of several small villages that went to make up the rest of the principality.

With every twist and turn of the road the charming clusters of flower-covered Italian villas and greenery enchanted Alex, who wasn't used to this kind of exercise to get about. What she'd gleaned from Lucca told her the country derived most of its income from tourism. She could see why. Between its beauty and the perfumed air, this had to be the most glorious place on earth.

Alex paused for a moment to take in the spectacular scenery. No wonder her mother had spent part of her honeymoon here. Who would ever have imagined Alex ending up being engaged to the prince of its ruling family?

It's all because of you, Mother.

And her father. She couldn't forget him.

The name "Grigory" had transformed Alex from a commoner to someone Lucca could present to his parents. In her case "a rose by any other name" would *not* smell as sweet. An accident of birth had made all the difference. Without it Lucca would never have decided to break in on her meeting with Mr. Defore.

Without her mother's diamonds being facsimiles of the real thing, Alex wouldn't have created the disturbance that had caught Lucca's attention in the first place.

Two desperate people from two unrelated worlds colliding in the cosmos at the critical moment in time, for both of them. One minute earlier or later and there wouldn't have been impact. They would have hurtled on by without the slightest knowledge of the other one.

She swallowed hard. Already it was impossible to contemplate a world without Lucca in it. The realization terrified her, and she started walking faster. Before long she reached the inner district of the prosperous city bursting with boutiques, sidewalk cafés, art galleries, restaurants, souvenir shops and jewelry boutiques. The display of diamonds attracted droves of people milling about from every country in the world.

Alex entered one of the crowded souvenir shops. By the time it came her turn to check out with one of her traveler's cheques, she'd loaded up with a map of the Principality of Castelmare, a tiny Italian-English phrase book and a picture book on Castelmare's House of Savoy from past to present printed in Italian. There were photos of Lucca and his family. She couldn't wait to study them.

Two doors up she spied a restaurant. The delicious smells coming from inside made her realize she was hungry. When she checked her watch, she was surprised to discover it was quarter to eight. With the sun setting later, she'd been deceived into thinking it was much earlier.

Better eat now. No way would she go back to the palace and ask for a meal, but this place was packed. She stood around with her packages waiting for someone to leave.

"*Mademoiselle? Signorina?* Miss?" a male voice called to her.

For a while she ignored the guy sitting in one of the crowded booths, but he persisted in trying to get her attention. Finally she looked over at him. He was with a bunch of college-aged guys and girls talking and laughing.

The student singling her out could be one of any number of dark-haired Mediterranean types. Obviously there was room for one more in the booth. He stood up and made an extravagant gesture for her to sit down. Soon everyone was beckoning her over.

Why not? She was hungry and tired.

"Thank you," she said as he took her sack from her and put it under the table by her legs. He had an inviting smile and was just her height.

"Hello," everyone said with their heavy Italian accents. The friendly crowd proceeded to introduce themselves.

"My name is Fabbio."

"I'm Alex."

He frowned. "You have man's name?"

"It's short for Alexandra."

"Ah…very classy." Alex chuckled. "My English is not good?"

"It's very good. My Italian's terrible. Have you eaten here before?"

"*Si.*"

"What's that called?" She stared at his meal.

"Pasta."

She could see that.

"You like?"

"Yes."

"I get it for you." He called to the waiter, and before long a plate of hot pasta with potatoes and beans was placed in front of her. While they all conversed in spates of Italian, then English, she ate her dinner. Her first mouthful was so delicious she consumed everything in short order. The five of them shared a bottle of wine. He poured her a glass. "Drink."

"Thank you very much."

The fruity flavored rosé served for her dessert. She hadn't had a glass of wine in years. This was the perfect setting for it.

He pulled a flier out of his pocket. "You want to come?" She took a look at it. Some kind of concert was being held in the city. Before she could turn him down she heard footsteps coming closer, then a deep male voice said, "*Bellissima*—I'm sorry I'm late."

The whole restaurant went silent.

Her head whipped around in time to see Lucca standing there in the same clothes he'd had on earlier, but he was wearing sunglasses. A gasp escaped her throat. He was supposed to be with someone else. At least, that was why she'd left the palace in the first place, so he could go to her.

Alex was so shocked to see him here, her mouth went dry. She couldn't get any words out. Neither could the clientele who had recognized the crown prince and were obviously stunned to see him walk in here of all places.

Before she could credit it, Lucca lowered his mouth to hers in what could only be construed as a possessive kiss, urgently coaxing her lips apart. Caught off guard she welcomed the electrifying invasion of that incredibly male mouth. Her body reeled in response.

Scarcely aware of what was happening, she realized he'd pulled some Euros from his wallet and put them on the table. Still speaking English he said to the others, "Enjoy the concert."

In a lightning move he retrieved her sack from beneath

the table. Her body couldn't stop weaving from the excitement of his kiss as he helped her to her feet. She smiled at Fabbio. "Thank you for being so nice to a stranger."

He nodded, still tongue-tied.

Lucca escorted her from the restaurant. A black limo stood parked outside. The net of bodyguards had increased. She thought Carlo gave her a frown before Lucca climbed in the back next to her and shut the door behind him.

Halfway to the palace she couldn't stand the silence any longer. "Obviously, I don't know all the rules yet, but was it absolutely necessary for you to do what you did just now?"

"I'm afraid so," he muttered in an oblique tone. "In three weeks the world will know you're my wife, but those students will remember that you went into the restaurant unaccompanied and responded to an invitation to sit with them. I'm aware you accepted because there was no other place available, but from their point of view you looked and acted like you welcomed his attention.

"I wouldn't want the incident, no matter how inconsequential it might have seemed in your eyes, to reach my parents' ears."

"Of course not." She felt sick inside. "I honestly didn't think. Forgive me, Lucca. I promise it won't ever happen again."

He extended his legs and crossed his arms. "It'll happen again and again because you're the kind of woman a man can't forget. From now on, all you have to do when you're out by yourself for any reason is to remember that you're already taken. Let the interested party know where he stands before he weaves fantasies about being alone with you."

"No man has ever had dreams about me."

"That's not what one of your bodyguards reported.

Apparently the young boy and his friends had a bet to see how long it would take him to bed the goddess standing inside the doorway."

Her cheeks went crimson. "Then the bodyguard made it up!"

"A lie to me could cost him his job and worse."

Alex shivered. "It was all a big mistake. I shopped too long and then I got hungry."

"You could have eaten at the palace. That's your home now."

"But I didn't want to bother anyone this late."

Instead of commenting, he asked a question. "How did you like your *trenette?*"

"Trenette?"

"It's what you had for dinner. Pasta Ligurian style."

"Oh…I loved it!"

"Bene."

She darted him a furtive glance. "Your parents will probably hear about my big faux pas and consider me unfit to be your wife. They'd be right!"

"I'll tell them about it as soon as we get back to the palace, then it won't matter when they hear it distorted on the news."

Alex let out a small cry. She was a fool, just like her mother whose antics were made into the news every night of the week.

"Like parasites, the paparazzi live on their hosts. Over the years I've learned the best defense is offense," he explained.

She stared at her hands. "How will you explain about my being in town without you?"

"The truth always helps. I'll tell them I had a lot of business and you didn't want to bother me on my first day home. You went exploring in town and stopped for something to eat, unaware some man had his sights set on you. Tomorrow Papa will remind you that you're not in America now. Mama will laugh and accuse me of being jealous. The whole incident will be forgotten."

Maybe, but Alex knew Lucca could never be jealous. He would have to be in love with Alex for that to happen.

"Let's hope."

He reached for her sack. "I wonder what you bought."

She was afraid he would laugh. "Touristy things. Didn't my bodyguards tell you?"

His expression remained impassive. "They'll only report if you're in danger." A sobering thought. "May I see?"

Since he appeared so determined, she didn't try to stop him. "Go ahead."

The book came out first. "This isn't the best history," he pointed out seconds later, "but it's not the worst, either."

"I wouldn't know, since I can't read Italian yet. I bought it for the pictures."

He suddenly lifted his head and gave her a long, unsmiling look. "After the coronation and our marriage, a plethora of new books will appear in the shops. You'll be in every one of them and every account will say that Princess Alexandra is the most beautiful of all the brides of the House of Savoy."

Lucca could tell superb lies. She rolled her eyes. "If you insist."

His laughter helped dissipate her worry that he was upset with her for the second time since their arrival in his country.

He pulled out the next item and thumbed through it. "I approve of your pocket phrase book. It's how I began to learn English."

For some reason his comment reassured her.

After scanning the map, he said, "This needs a little help. I'll fix it when we get back to the palace." He returned everything to the sack. "I noticed you're not wearing my pin."

"No. It's too precious to flaunt."

He grasped her hand, entwining their fingers. "You're my fiancée now. After what you told Regina, I couldn't very well give you an engagement ring. Wear the pin for me?"

"You mean, all the time?"

"Yes, all the time."

She sucked in her breath. "If you wish."

"Is it such a burden?" he whispered.

"Lucca—surely you understand the worry I have about losing it. The stone is irreplaceable."

"What good is it if it's never worn?"

"You really feel strongly about this, don't you?"

"Yes."

"All right," her voice trembled.

"Grazie."

The limo pulled to a stop beneath the north portico of the palace. Lucca cupped her elbow and ushered her inside. They parted company at the second floor.

"Buonanotte, Alexandra." After pressing a light, unexpected kiss to her parted lips, he strode swiftly toward his parents' suite. She knew he was on his way to put out a fire the media would have started.

Little did he know the damage he'd done to her at the restaurant. That deeply searching kiss for the crowd's benefit had fanned the flames of a conflagration growing inside her with no power to contain it.

CHAPTER SIX

Lucca checked his watch. Five to twelve. Alexandra's first day of learning Italian with Professor Emilio ought to be over by now. He was retired from the university, but according to Regina, the older man still did tutoring.

He left his palace office on the main floor and hurried up the steps to the third floor where the schoolroom was located, but his excitement dissipated when he opened the door and heard Alex laughing quietly with a man who couldn't be much older than Lucca.

The sight of the two of them enjoying each other's company in this intimate atmosphere shook him to the roots, something that hadn't happened to him before where a woman was concerned.

One look at the tutor's face and body language and Lucca knew Alexandra had him enchanted just as she'd done that idiot college kid at the restaurant last night. It didn't take a two-hour lesson for her to work her magic. Lucca ought to know because to his great surprise, it was beginning to work on him.

She was dressed in the familiar plum silk shirt and gray pants he'd admired before. After lunch he had plans to do something about her bare-bones wardrobe, but at the moment the only thing Lucca was feeling was irrationally territorial.

He moved inside.

The other man saw him before Alexandra did. He slid off the corner of the desk and stood up. The fact that he was lean and almost as tall as Lucca irritated him further.

"Your Highness."

Alexandra turned in her chair. "Lucca—"

He couldn't tell if she was pleased to see him or not, but she was wearing his pin. That was something at least and should have appeased him. It didn't.

She got to her feet, very much in command of the situation. "Lucca? This is Professor Morelli. Professor Emilio is ill so he sent Tomaso in his place."

Lucca gave Tomaso a brief nod. "I'm sorry to hear that. How long will it take him to recover?"

"He has influenza. His doctor says two weeks, maybe a little longer."

That was too long.

"How is my wife-to-be doing?" *Besides giving you a heart attack.* Lucca ground his teeth together. Wife-to-be sounded more permanent than fiancée. He wanted that made clear to Tomaso at the outset.

"Signorina Grigory is an excellent student. By the time of your wedding she'll be speaking a little Italian and understanding some of it."

She smiled. "One lives in hope, Tomaso. Thank you for taking me on."

"It's an honor for me."

And a rush you won't be able to do a thing in hell about, professor.

"I'll see you tomorrow."

Alexandra nodded. *"Si. Domani. Ore due. Ciao, Tomaso."*

"Ciao, Alex."

The hackles stood on the back of his neck. *Alex?* She'd given him permission to call her that?

His gaze slid to Lucca. "Your Highness," he said in passing.

"Why two o'clock?" Lucca asked after the other man had left the room.

She picked up the book and notebook he hadn't seen before. "Tomaso teaches classes all morning, but he can come after lunch. If I'd had a teacher like him for Spanish in high school, I might have learned how to conjugate verbs."

Intrigued in spite of his foul mood he asked, "What was wrong with your Spanish teacher?"

"He taught by immersion, and no one ever understood anything. He gave everyone an A for trying. It was ridiculous."

Laughter burst out of him. "What verb did Professor Morelli teach you to conjugate today?"

"To be. *Essere. Io sono, tu sei, lui e, noi siamo, voi siete, loro sono.*"

"I'm impressed." He was more than impressed. Her little conversation a moment ago sounded as if she'd been studying a lot longer than two hours.

"He said I have good pronunciation. Do you think he was just saying that to make me feel better?" Lucca realized she wasn't fishing for compliments. She really wanted to know. It dawned on him she really was a good woman, someone he would be proud to call his wife.

"I told you the other day you have an excellent ear. Why do you doubt it?"

She averted her eyes. "I don't know."

Lucca knew. Alexandra's mother had never given her confidence. Considering her father had died in her infancy, it was a miracle she had any at all. Fate had made her strong, courageous. Lucca had plans to fill in the rest. The thought of it taking a lifetime lightened his spirits.

"Come on. I'm taking you to lunch at a favorite restaurant of mine."

"Oh, good!" Her seductive mouth smiled as they left the room, giving him his reward. "Tomaso taught me some phrases to practice when I order. We went over the names of the basic foods."

Diavolo!

She turned to him. "Did you say something?"

"Nothing worth repeating."

Her eyes played over his features. "You sound a bit like snappy turtle today."

"Snappy turtle?" he barked with barely suppressed amusement.

"You know. A little cross. With all you're taking on, I don't blame you. How can I help?"

He drew in a deep breath. "Just be with me today."

"Your wish is my command, Your Highness."

"I asked you not to say that."

A pained expression crossed over her face. "I'm sorry. It came out before I realized it. I really wasn't thinking of you in that sense. I believe you're emotionally exhausted, Lucca."

Without conscious thought he put his arms around her and pulled her close. Burying his face in her sweet smelling hair he whispered, "I think you know me better than I know myself."

"That's what arranged wives are for." *And this one-to-be knows exactly what is ailing you.*

Again Alex had spoken freely, not weighing her words beforehand. When he held her like this, she forgot the reason she was here at all. The desire to kiss his sensual mouth and go on kissing it the way she'd wanted to at the restaurant was turning into a driving need, blinding her to common sense.

The only reason he didn't feel the same urge was because someone else was in his thoughts, someone he couldn't wait to be with on a permanent basis. In a curious way he needed Alex. Almost overnight they'd become friends. She understood that and didn't read into the moment that it was emotional for him.

"I have an idea." Though it was the last thing she wanted to do, she slowly eased out of his arms. "After we eat lunch, why don't you give yourself permission to take time off and do what you really want to do until tomorrow."

He studied her through veiled eyes. "That's excellent advice. Shall we go?"

Apparently, she'd said the magic words. He was planning to act on her suggestion. Another shaft of pain splintered her heart. *Get used to it, Alex.*

When they reached the second floor, he turned to her. "Meet me at the north portico in five minutes."

"I'll be there." She hurried down the hall to her suite, tossing her Italian book and notebook on the bed. Once she'd washed her face and brushed her hair, she grabbed her purse and flew out the door.

"Ciao, Alexandra." Lucca's sister was just coming out of her room.

She drew to a halt. *"Ciao, Regina."*

She smiled. "How did the Italian lesson go?"

"I loved it."

"Good. Where are you off to in such a hurry now?"

"Lucca and I are going out for lunch."

Her brown eyes smiled. "I was about to ask if you'd like to have a meal in town with me, but I can see you have a much more pressing engagement."

Alex liked Regina and wanted to include her, even though she was looking forward to being alone with Lucca. "Why don't we all go together?"

Regina shook her head. "If my brother had wanted me along, he would have asked me. Go and enjoy yourselves."

"You're sure? Come with me and we'll ask him."

"His favorite car only fits two."

"Maybe we're going in the limo."

"I doubt it."

"Then you can squeeze in with us."

After a gentle laugh she put a hand on Alex's arm. "I believe you *would* make room for me, but under the circumstances I'm going to check on my parents. Have a lovely outing."

"Grazie, Regina." She'd practiced it with Tomaso. It was one of the Italian words she loved to say.

"Prego, Alexandra."

They walked together, then parted company at the stairway. Alex felt like flying down it, but since it would look as if she couldn't wait to be with Lucca, she controlled herself and descended as gracefully as she knew how.

It would be good practice for their wedding day, when she had to walk up and down the front steps of the cathedral she'd passed in town last evening. What would she do if she fell flat on her face?

Lucca was waiting for her at the entrance, but his expression darkened as she drew closer. "Tell me what's put that worried look in your eyes. Something's happened."

The man's radar didn't miss anything. "No." She shook her head. "I was thinking how awful it would be to trip on the steps of the cathedral in my wedding dress."

His taut body relaxed. "Should that occur, everyone would feel better for knowing you're human, too. If anything, you would endear yourself to the crowd."

She stared at him. "Were you born a diplomat or did you learn it from your parents through osmosis?"

His lips twitched as he put a hand behind her waist and ushered her out the doors to a black Ferrari. Once inside his sensational car, he helped her fasten the seat belt. Too much bodily contact within the elegant leather confines set her trembling.

"My parents will tell you I was born a hellion and will probably go out of this world the same way." As they sped away from the palace, she acknowledged he drove like one.

Every woman loved a bad boy. Wasn't that the collective opinion?

Alex had to admit, it was Lucca's wild side that made him the bigger-than-life, exciting male who'd overcome every obstacle to get her on that plane. No ordinary man could have managed it.

She still couldn't comprehend how it had happened. All she knew for a certainty was that in a little over two days she'd fallen hopelessly in love with him.

"I met Regina in the hall and asked her to come with us, but she declined."

"Smart girl," he quipped.

Alex smiled to herself. "She's such a natural person. I like her very much."

"So do I."

They wound up the hillside behind Capriccio and on through a town called Savono. With every kilometer the traffic thinned until they came to a tiny hamlet nestled beneath a mountaintop. It looked ancient, almost untouched by time. Forgotten even.

Lucca pulled to a stop in front of a stone church in partial ruin. No one was about. His bodyguards were doing an amazing job of keeping the paparazzi at bay.

"This is Dirupo. The word means crag, the northern-most boundary of Castelmare. Historians say it came into being in the twelfth century. There's one grocery store with a bank and post office inside. The inn only has twelve rooms."

"This place has a lonely feel, doesn't it, yet that's the reason for its charm," Alex murmured. She got out of the car to look around. There was a plaque on one of the church's stones with an explanation in four languages. She read the English version with interest. He joined her.

"I thought the same thing when I first explored up here as a boy. Right now it's on a long list of things to be discussed at the cabinet meeting tomorrow. Several of the ministers want to allow hotels and restaurants to be built up here to bring in more tourism. Because of the mountain streams they're talking of creating a spa. Yet others argue it will destroy the watershed."

She drew in a deep breath. "The view of the Mediterranean is unmatched, Lucca. Tourists would kill to vacation in a spot like this. You could charge a fortune for a one-night stay."

Alex continued to look out at the spectacular view. Being with him filled her with feelings of euphoria. "On the other hand it could be overrun and lose the bit of history that makes it so unique. There aren't many untouched places like this left in the world...."

Lucca's gaze wandered over her features. "I knew if I brought you up here, I'd be able to resolve it in my mind."

For no good reason her heart rate sped up. "What have you concluded?"

"I'm going to suggest we put a moratorium on any building, but we'll restore the church and any existing structures needing repair work."

She smiled at him. "Two hundred years from now your country will praise you for your vision."

He cocked his head. "You think I want praise?"

"In the best sense, yes. If I were a monarch, I would like to think I'd left a legacy that preserved a vital slice of the country's origins. Otherwise what would people in the future have to look forward to?"

Lucca seemed to ponder her comment before he said, "You've just helped me write the essence of my coronation speech. For that gift I'm going to take you inside the inn and buy you a lunch of fresh brook trout that will melt in your mouth."

By now she was famished. "How do you say trout?"

"Trota di fiume."

"Do you mind if I order for us?"

He reached for her hand and they started walking toward the entrance. "I'm planning on it."

"I promised Tomaso I would take advantage of every opportunity."

His hand seemed to tighten around her fingers before he let it go long enough to open the door for her. "After we eat, we'll stop by the cathedral to visit with the archbishop.

The banns have to go out for our marriage. Then we'll buy you some clothes for tomorrow."

She gulped. "Why? I thought we were going to wait until my belongings arrived."

"There's no time. My father has already put things in motion. In the morning before the cabinet meeting at ten, the journalists from the major American and European television networks will come to the palace to broadcast the official news of the upcoming coronation and our marriage. I'll be at your side the entire time and field any difficult questions."

Her jaw hardened. "You mean, about me following in my mother's footsteps."

He lifted a wayward curl off her forehead. "Love is no respecter of persons past or present. Everyone has an equal right to it with whomever and wherever they find it."

Except for a prince who must do his duty.

Two hours later his words were still revolving in her head as they entered an exclusive boutique in Capriccio where, Lucca told her, his mother and sister often shopped.

The clerk who waited on them recognized him, of course. When Lucca explained what they wanted, she told him she had the perfect outfit for Alex, who was still replete from their delicious meal.

Within seconds the woman produced a knee-length dress of woven lightweight silk in a heavenly shade of oyster. The diamond pin would look fabulous against it. As soon as Alex slipped it on, she had to admit the jewel neckline and tiered short sleeves suited her tall, softly rounded figure.

Lucca said as much when she left the fitting room and

modeled it for him. His searching gaze started at her feet and made a slow, intimate perusal of her body. By the time it reached her face, her cheeks were on fire.

"The color of the material matches your eyes." His gaze flicked to the clerk. "We'll take it and some other outfits for day and evening. She'll need shoes and lingerie." On that note he refocused his attention on Alex. "Take your time, *bellissima*. We're in no hurry."

When Alex was a child, she used to pretend she'd been let loose in a store and could have anything she wanted. It felt like that now. After agreeing to marry him she couldn't keep going around in the same two outfits. The clothes being shipped might not arrive for weeks and probably wouldn't be appropriate for many future occasions, anyway. Naturally he wanted to be proud of her.

For once she decided to take him at his word. Unfortunately, she had so much fun they didn't get out of there until it was close to 6:00 p.m. The clerk told her the packages would be delivered to the palace by eight. It was embarrassingly late already and Lucca had been sitting there for hours!

So much for letting him have time alone with his lover this afternoon. Red-faced, she apologized. "I'm sorry I took so long."

"I'm not. This has helped me get my mind off affairs of state. I don't remember the last time I felt this relaxed." He got to his feet. "You're good for me, Alexandra."

She sobered. "Thank you for being so generous. I promise to pa—" but nothing else came out because he silenced her with his lips.

"No talk of repaying me now or ever," he whispered.

Alex had said the wrong thing again, but she had to

remember that when they were out in public, his actions were always orchestrated to convince their audience he was in love. "I promise," she whispered back, but she did intend to repay him one day. She just wouldn't talk about it.

They left the boutique through the back door, where he'd parked his car. His security people had set up a barricade on the tiny street to give them space, but people pressed against it, eager for a glimpse of the prince.

Lucca had grown up learning how to handle the public. No matter where they went or what they did, he didn't seem to give them any thought. Alex wondered how long it would take her not to feel like she was a goldfish on display.

The crowded streets made it impossible for Lucca to zip back to the palace at warp speed, but she gave him credit for trying. "Home at last and in one piece," he drawled after shutting off the powerful engine.

"At last?" she teased. "A fighter jet couldn't have arrived here any sooner."

Suddenly he looked repentant. "Alexandra— I forgot about the helicopter. I should have requested it—"

"Don't apologize," she cut him off. "It was the events of the day that knocked me off balance, not the lack of a helicopter. The truth is, I found out in New York you only function at high speed. I like speed, too. If I owned a car like this, I'd be banned from driving it after the first time I went around the block."

His hand slid from the gearshift to her lower thigh, sending out one heatwave after another. "Next week I'll take you to a track in Monaco where you can let it rip to your heart's content."

"You'd let me drive this?"

His gaze sobered. "Of course. I don't think you understand yet. Everything I have is yours." After squeezing her leg gently he levered himself from the driver's seat and came around to help her. She was glad she was wearing pants. With her long limbs it would be impossible to keep them modestly covered while trying to climb out under his all-seeing eye.

"How much time do you need to freshen up?" he asked once they'd reached the second floor.

Surely he wanted to get away on his own, but being the dutiful prince, he felt he owed her his time in order to look like the attentive fiancé. Today he'd done more than any engaged woman could ask for. Now it was up to her to return the favor.

"Since I'm going to have to face my first press conference in the morning, I'd prefer to have an early night, but in case you need me in an official capacity, I can be ready whenever you want."

A remote expression crossed over his masculine features. There was a pause. "What I had in mind can wait."

Of course it could. His thoughts were on his lover. They'd been apart long enough.

"Then if you don't mind, I'll ask the kitchen to send up a sandwich while I get started on my writing exercises for Tomaso."

On impulse she kissed his hard-boned jaw where she could feel the beginnings of his beard. Another enticement she mustn't dwell on. "Thank you for a wonderful day. I'll always remember it. *Buonanotte,* Lucca."

"I'll come by your room at quarter past nine in the morning. *Sogni d'oro,* Alexandra."

Tomorrow she would have to ask Tomaso what it meant.

* * *

Lucca spent a restless night tossing and turning. Her last words to him before running off sounded like a goodbye speech, and they weren't even married yet. She was more excited about her next Italian lesson than being with him.

He couldn't fault her for anything where their agreement was concerned. Her performance so far was nothing short of miraculous. Unfortunately, he found himself wanting more from her. Because his feelings for her were growing, it was probably just as well he'd been forced to come back to his room and take a cold shower.

She was right about him. He didn't know how to take things slow, but it appeared that for once in his life he was going to have to learn that lesson. In the past few days he'd come to realize his whole life's happiness depended on it.

At eight the next morning, he and Regina ate breakfast in his parents' suite. By nine o'clock he'd showered and shaved. At 9:10 a.m. he left his suite wearing a dark gray business suit and tie. Aware his need to see Alexandra was over the top, he had to tamp down his excitement, but he couldn't prevent the explosion of his senses when she opened the door to him, the embodiment of feminine allure.

Her silver high heels added two inches, making it easier for him to capture that supple mouth wearing a light pink frost. He almost acted on his desire to taste her, but remembering who was waiting for them downstairs, he caught himself in time.

If his eyes didn't deceive him, her heart was pounding faster than normal. The diamond seemed to be in constant motion, pulsating with bursts of green light. Each beat matched the rhythm of his own heart, increasing in speed like his Ferrari.

She raised those solemn gray eyes to his. "Do I look all

right? I wouldn't want to embarrass you." Her freshly washed hair smelled of peaches, a scent he would always associate with her.

The thing about Alexandra was that she didn't have one selfish, self-absorbed, narcissistic atom in her body.

"You'll do," was all he could manage to say. In an automatic gesture he grasped her hand, twining his fingers around hers as they started down the hall.

"Where are we going?"

"To the conference room of my office on the main floor."

She flashed him an anxious glance. "You don't show it, but are you scared? Just a little bit?"

He took a steadying breath. "I was a lot scared until you opened your door just now." If she hadn't been there… If she'd run away because she couldn't go through with it after all…

"You always say and do the right thing, Lucca. Thank you for sending the manicurist and hair dresser. My nails needed help, but I'm afraid my hair is hopeless."

"I like your hair exactly the way it is. As for your nails, I've never noticed. Mama saw to those details this morning."

"Then I'll have to thank her later. Has your father forgiven me for the other night?"

"Since I'm not exactly the poster boy of perfection, either, he said your escapade convinced him we're made for each other."

"That's not very reassuring."

Lucca chuckled before giving in to the urge to kiss her neck. "All in all, we're off to a better start than I would have imagined." Just getting her to Castelmare had been a feat.

Once they reached the main floor, he caught hold of her upper arms. "You'll see a lot of government officials in there.

Don't let it bother you. Their presence will help keep the news conference civilized. Remember you're half Carlisle, half Grigory, a unique combination unlike any other."

She gave a meek nod.

He cupped her chin and raised it a trifle. "One more thing. Keep your eyes on me."

"I already planned on doing that," came her quiet response.

Their mouths were only centimeters apart. Unable to help himself, he gave a quick kiss to those pliant lips, uncaring that some of her lipstick stayed on his...a little part of her he could savor until the day came when he would taste all of her.

Carlo cleared his throat behind them. "Everyone's waiting."

"Ready?" Lucca asked her. They stared into each other's eyes for a moment. Hers were guarded. Then she surprised him by lifting her hand to wipe the lipstick off his mouth with her fingers.

"Now I am."

It reminded him of the things his mother did for his father before an important dinner or conference so he would look his best. Alexandra could have no idea how the small gesture moved him.

Binding her hand to his once more, he drew her toward the west end of the palace where the double doors of the conference room were opened wide. The buzz of voices filtered down the hall.

The president of the cabinet was officiating today. He stood at the lectern placed on a raised platform in the center of the room. Everyone was seated below him. Regina sat to the side of the lectern representing Lucca's immediate family. As soon as the statesman saw Lucca, he struck a staff to the floor several times.

"Ladies and gentlemen of the press, members of the cabinet, His Royal Highness, the Crown Prince Lucca Umberto Schiaparelli Vittorio the Fifth of Castelmare and the Princess Alexandra Carlisle Grigory."

Everyone rose to their feet and began clapping. Amidst the cheers came the inevitable shower of flashbulbs going off.

For Lucca it was a source of intense personal pride that Alexandra handled it as though she'd been born to it. All his life he'd dreaded this day coming, but that was before Alex....

CHAPTER SEVEN

KEEP your eyes on Lucca. Like a mantra Alex repeated his advice.

The huge room, as ornate and splendid as the rest of the palace, had to be filled with several hundred people if you included all the security assembled. Regina, looking beautiful in a dusky-rose suit, gloves and a broad-brimmed hat with a cluster of real roses at the side of the crown, sent her a private smile.

Alex reciprocated before ascending the platform with Lucca. A dozen microphones had been set up to carry the broadcast. It was the middle of the night in Los Angeles. By morning Alex's friends would see all this on TV at work and go into shock. Before the end of the day she would have to make phone calls of explanation to them and Mr. Watkins.

Unfortunately, she couldn't tell anyone the truth in case it ended up hurting Lucca. All she could say was that Lucca was responsible for helping her unite with her family and in the process he'd swept her off her feet.

Any woman seeing Lucca would understand how that could happen. Anyone catching sight of the green diamond fastened to her dress would agree that Alex was as greedy as her mother.

Yet strangely enough, none of it stung, because she had Lucca on her side. They'd entered into a pact to help each other. With him championing her, she had nothing to fear except an inability to get into medical school. But she wouldn't think in defeatist terms. Right now her only job was to play Lucca's adoring fiancée in front of the camcorders, a role she found came as naturally to her as breathing.

After the head of the cabinet sat down, Lucca moved to the lectern taking Alex with him. Together they faced the sea of faces.

"Ladies and gentlemen of the press, translators, members of the cabinet and their assistants," he began in English, "I've called this news conference to announce my ascendancy to the throne on the twenty-eighth of this month. My father's health demands that he step down." Lucca's voice broke, revealing the depth of his concern for his parent. In the stillness following his news, Alex slid her hand into his. He gripped it so hard, he had no idea of his strength.

"As all of you can see, I picked up something precious while I was in New York. Alexandra has consented to become my wife. Regretfully, her father, Prince Oleg Grigory, and her mother, Kathryn Carlisle, are both deceased. But it's most fortunate that her great-uncle Yuri Grigory is still alive and will walk her down the aisle.

"My parents have declared the twenty-eighth of this month a state holiday in honor of the coronation and my wedding to this wonderful woman." He lifted her hand and kissed the back of it. The barrage of flashes almost blinded her.

"Before the cabinet meeting starts, Alexandra and I will entertain a few questions now."

Too many voices called out at once. "One at a time please," Lucca said with enviable calm.

"Princess Alexandra, how does it feel to be wearing the Ligurian teardrop diamond?"

Lucca darted her an amused glance, obviously curious to know what she was going to say.

"Like I'm carrying a monument around." Her comment set off an explosion of laughter in the room that included Lucca's own deep, attractive brand. It took a minute for the noise to subside.

"Princess Alexandra?" came another voice. "How did you manage to keep your involvement with the prince a secret all this time?"

"I have my ways." Taking a risk she added, "My mother was always in the news. I learned certain tricks to remain invisible."

"Over here, Princess Alexandra—" This from a burly journalist in the corner. "Rumor has it your father had ties to the mafia in Las Vegas. Can you confirm that?"

Lucca stiffened. She could tell he was ready to intervene but she preempted him.

"Yes," she spoke clearly. "It was rumor. My father was an excellent businessman who used his own money to be successful. Sadly, his life was cut short in an airplane crash. I would give anything if he were still alive." Her voice shook.

A strong arm slipped around her waist, pulling her closer, then Lucca said, "One last question."

"Princess Alexandra?" This from an older woman journalist. "It's obvious that like your mother you could have your choice of many men, be they sheiks, royals or film stars." That was news to Alex. "What was it about Prince Lucca you couldn't resist?"

Alex needed to put on a convincing act, but it wasn't hard. She slowly smiled at him. "We met while I was in a shop. At first I mistook him for a security guard. I was in a very anxious state at the time and I'm afraid I unfairly took it out on one of the employees.

"When Lucca intervened, I assumed he'd been watching and had decided to take charge. We exchanged words. Actually I flung insults at him and demanded to know if he was going to have me arrested. In his maddeningly reasonable way he assured me nothing could be further from the truth and suggested I sit down. Now when I look back on the incident, I realize he'd used his monarch voice on me."

Laughter burst from the audience. Lucca eyed her with a devilish gleam.

"The man had so much charm that before long I discovered I was having the time of my life. When he finally admitted who he was, I'm afraid I was hooked." At this point she fought to keep her voice steady.

"I say afraid because I didn't want him to be a prince, but once the heart feels that pull, you have no choice in the matter. He more or less took me away, but not to prison, thank heaven. Of course, the fact that he was easily the most attractive man I'd ever met didn't hurt the situation any."

Everyone jumped to their feet cheering and clapping their approval, but not Lucca. He studied her out of dark, veiled eyes, his expression suddenly indecipherable. Had she said too much? Was he worried what his lover would make of it?

Honesty was usually the best policy, but maybe not in this case. Her off-the-cuff speech would be circling the world before long. It was too late to recall it.

Lucca let go of her hand and put both of his on the lectern. "As you have deduced," he began in his deep voice, "our marriage is going to be a lively, twenty-first-century version of thrills."

The crowd gave them a standing ovation. He waited for the din to subside before he said, "I want to thank those members of the media for coming. Because of the cabinet's urgent business now that my father is stepping down, we would appreciate it if you cleared the conference room so our meeting can begin."

On cue the cameramen and reporters started to exit the room. While the president of the cabinet engaged Lucca in conversation, Regina came running up to Alex. "You were wonderful," she whispered, catching hold of her arm.

Alex hadn't seen her leave her seat. "Thanks, Regina, but I'm afraid I said too much."

"No. It was perfect!" she argued. "I've been dying to learn how you met, but you know my close-mouthed brother. I saw everyone's reaction, Alexandra. They love you. *I* love you for loving my brother so much. He badly needs to be loved by a woman like you."

Lucca was already badly loved by a woman, but Regina didn't know that. However, the sincerity of her words made Alex realize she'd pulled off her part of the agreement with Lucca. If Regina could accept they were a love match, then she wasn't worried about other people.

"Come on," Regina urged. "Papa and Mama asked me to bring you to their suite after the news conference. Lucca will be tied up all day."

That's what Alex feared. The hours dragged when she wasn't with him. "All right."

"Lucca?" she called to her brother who was busy talking to several men by now. He turned his head in their direction. "We're going upstairs."

"I'll join you later." His glance swerved to Alex. She saw a nerve throbbing at the corner of his jaw. "You had them eating out of your hand, Alexandra."

Then why aren't you happy about it? Alex didn't understand his unexpected change of mood, but she couldn't ask him about it. At this juncture the press of dignitaries surrounding him had grown.

Averting her eyes, she turned her attention back to Regina. They left through a private door at the rear of the room. "After we've checked in with my parents, I thought you might like a tour of the grounds."

"I'd love it, but I have another Italian lesson at two with Professor Morelli."

"There'll be time for both." She gave Alex a sideways glance. "I saw him on the stairs after he left the schoolroom yesterday. Apparently Professor Emilio is ill."

"That's what I understand."

"He's very nice looking."

Alex smiled. "I agree. He's a terrific teacher, too."

One of Regina's brows lifted. "Does Lucca know about the change?"

"Yes."

"Ah, that explains it."

"Explains what?" Alex prodded.

"Lucca's mood at breakfast after Mama asked if you'd begun your Italian lessons. He didn't seem to want to talk about it."

"You know he did seem a little offish after I introduced him to Tomaso. I assumed he was disappointed Professor Emilio couldn't make it."

A knowing smile broke out on Regina's face. "My brother's jealous."

"Don't be silly, Regina. I've done nothing to make him feel that way."

"You don't have to. It's an emotion completely new to him. I love seeing him out of control for once."

Alex couldn't afford to protest too much. "I think you're wrong."

"Better not refer to Professor Morelli as Tomaso in front of him," she said.

"Does that mean I'm breaking some kind of royal protocol to address him by his first name?"

"Of course not, but you don't know my brother like I do. At least not yet. He has a possessive streak about certain things he considers his."

"I *am* his," she blurted. Sort of. Come to think of it, he was pretty obsessed over her wearing his pin all the time.

"You and I both know that. However, to be safe I implore you to be formal with Tomaso in front of Lucca and whatever you do, don't praise your teacher. Lucca would never be able to handle it."

Alex broke into laughter. She couldn't help it, but Regina remained serious. "Laugh if you want, but don't say I didn't warn you."

At quarter to three that afternoon Alex was reminded of their conversation when Lucca came striding into the schoolroom unannounced. He was still dressed in the stunning gray suit he'd worn for the press conference. Her breath caught at the magnificent sight of him.

She'd been working on the next chapter in her Italian book while she waited for Tomaso. Evidently he'd been held up at the university and was running late.

"Hi," was all she could get out.

"Hi, yourself." He removed his elegant suit jacket and

flung it over a chair. Then he removed his tie and rolled up the sleeves of his immaculate white shirt to the elbow, revealing bronzed arms.

"P-Professor Morelli's late," she tripped over the word because she almost said Tomaso. "So I've just been studying."

Lucca sat down at the desk facing her. He flashed her a look of male admiration. She'd changed clothes and was wearing a soft orange linen wraparound dress he'd admired on her at the boutique. Her only adornment was the pin. "He won't be coming anymore. I'll instruct you every day until Professor Emilio is well enough to do it."

Joy.

Remembering Regina's warning, she said, "I'm glad because I'd rather be taught by you." Her comment seemed to smooth the waters a little. She took advantage of the silence. "How did the cabinet meeting go?"

"Fine," he answered, but she could tell his mind wasn't on government affairs. "Every man in the room envied me today."

"They can envy you all they want, but could any of them make as good a king?"

"You know damn well I wasn't referring to the title," his voice rasped.

Adrenaline gushed through her veins. "How do you say damn in Italian? I think I should learn some curse words. In the States all the foreigners can swear in English before they say anything else."

A quick smile transformed his chiseled features. "Like English, Italian has many subtleties," he said in a more relaxed tone. "You can say *managgia*. The slang for it is *accidenti*. A politer version is *diavolo*."

Her head flew back. "I heard you say that word the other day."

"So I did." He suddenly shoved himself away from the desk and stood up. "Let's get out of here. You can work on those words while we take a drive."

She rolled her eyes. "Something tells me they're going to come in handy."

He let out a bark of laughter before reaching for his coat and tie. "Have you ever ridden on the back of a motorcycle before?"

A thrill of excitement ran through her body. "No."

"You said you liked speed. I'm going to take you at your word."

Almost jumping out of her skin in anticipation, she hurried over to the door ahead of him. "I'll need to change first."

"Meet me in the north portico in ten minutes. Wear those blue jeans you bought yesterday. On our way out of town, we'll pick up the rest of the items you'll need."

"All right."

She reached her room breathless over their plans, but when she discovered all the phone messages waiting for her from the States, they brought her back to the grim reality that every gesture on Lucca's part was meant for show.

Outwardly he was carrying on his role as the ardent fiancé but she'd be a much greater fool than her mother if she allowed herself to stay in denial about his deepest feelings. There *was* another woman. He'd told her in the car on the way to airport.

In order not to displease his parents, Alex was beginning to think he intended to stay away from his lover until the honeymoon was over. When Lucca had talked about his work schedule, he'd told Alex that after he performed his royal duties each day, he would indulge his other interests. She'd known what he'd meant, but it was getting harder and harder to accept.

Deflated by the unpalatable truth about her deepest feelings, she checked each message. All of them could wait except the one from Manny. *SOS, Alex. Must talk to you immediately! Call me no matter what time it is! This could settle all your mother's debts and then some!*

Her heart thudded in her chest. How was that possible?

She quickly returned the call. He picked up on the second ring. "You're a good girl for calling me back so fast, Alex. How would you like to be a very, very rich one in no time at all?"

"Were mother's real diamonds found?" she cried.

"No, no, honey. Those are long gone."

Her brief elation dissipated. She sank down on the side of the bed. "Then I don't understand."

"Listen to me and don't interrupt. Can you do that?"

If she didn't get downstairs soon, Lucca would come looking for her. "Yes—if you make it quick. I'm on my way out the door."

"I've got the part of the century for you!"

She frowned. "What are you talking about, Manny?"

"Oh, honey, after seeing your beautiful face splashed all over the news and the Internet this morning, you're the only one who can play it."

"Play what?"

"*Garbo!* I've got the script in my hand. Every actress in Hollywood wants the part. None of them can do it. They don't have what it takes. You do! Come home, Alex. I've already got the audition arranged for you."

She shot to her feet. "Manny, I'm not an actress!"

"Ah, honey…you've been around it all your life."

It was hard to breathe. "If you saw me on TV, then you'd know I'm getting married."

"You can work around that. The point is, you can carry off the role so people will believe you're Garbo. I just talked to Michelle. She agrees with that me you've got those great bones—everything it takes including her sad eyes.

"Between your portrayal, plus the fact that you're Kathryn's daughter and the consort of Prince Vittorio of Castelmare, the box-office take will be *in the millions.* One film of the definitive Garbo, honey. Just one and you'll be on easy street for the rest of your life!"

And you'll get paid what mother owed you within the year instead of ten or twelve years from now.

For the first time in all these years, she was beginning to realize the kind of pressure her mother had lived under. Manny said and did all the right things. He was a master manipulator.

Alex's mind went back to the conversation with her Uncle Yuri:

"My mother was married six times," she'd said.

"I can understand why you're frightened. But think about this. Maybe part of it's because she lost Oleg, and maybe the other part is because she didn't have parents to teach her what a good marriage is all about. Hmm?" Yuri had told her.

There was a familiar rap on the door. "Alexandra?"

"I'll be right there, Lucca," she called out, then put the phone back to her ear. "Listen, Manny. I have to go."

"No way. Whatever else you have to do can wait."

She took a deep breath. "I'm afraid it can't, Manny. I'll have to call you later."

"When? This thing is big, honey. An opportunity like this only comes knocking once in a lifetime."

Manny never gave up!

Oh, Mother, he must have had you bound up so tightly, is it any wonder you tried to find escape with other men?

Her hand gripped the phone tighter. She could hardly concentrate for the knocking on the outer door, which was growing louder. "I realize that. Give me some time to think about it." She didn't want to hurt Manny, after all he was still waiting for his money. On the other hand she had to consider Lucca and the agreement she'd entered into with him. "I have to hang up now."

She dropped the phone on the receiver and ran through the suite. "Lucca? I need two more minutes."

"Are you all right?" he demanded.

"Y-yes."

"You don't sound it. Do you need help?"

"No…I'll be right there."

Alex half hopped out of her dress as she hurried to the dresser for the jeans and top she planned to wear. She'd barely slipped on her separates when Lucca entered her bedroom wearing jeans, a blue T-shirt beneath a black bomber-type leather jacket and riding boots. He looked fantastic.

"I'm not going to apologize for invading your privacy," he said worriedly, breathing hard. "You're as pale as parchment. After what you had to face this morning, it wouldn't surprise me if you're sick to your stomach. There's no way I'm taking you out on my motorcycle when you're ill."

Brushing a lock of hair off her forehead, she brazened out his intimate scrutiny. "I…I had a personal phone call I couldn't ignore," her voice faltered.

He folded his strong arms. His eyes glittered ominously. "Personal? From whom?"

"It was Manny, but it doesn't concern you. Like I said, it was personal."

"And might I ask who this Manny is who demands your attention but who is of no concern to me? Is he perhaps a former lover who saw you on the early-morning news in Los Angeles?"

"What?"

"Come on, Alexandra. You don't have to continue to lie to me. Clearly there is someone important in your life back home…a love interest—"

"I told you before there is no one. Thank you for having so much faith in me." She let the sarcasm fly.

He stared her down. "Today we told the whole world we're going to be married. I have a right to know who the man is who could change your entire countenance in an instant."

"Why is it you have to know *his* name when you haven't felt inclined to divulge *your* lover's name to me? I thought you trusted me, or isn't our marriage going to be on an equal footing after all? Wasn't it you who said no secrets?"

When his gaze slid away from hers, Alex knew she had him, but it gave her no joy. She sat down in the nearest up-holstered chair. "I thought we could be friends, Lucca. The last thing I want to do is fight with you."

The tension between them was combustible. "How long have you known him?"

"A long time, but it's not what you think." She didn't want to tell him about this. Not today of all days.

"It never is," he ground out.

She shook her head in bewilderment. "For the sake of

argument, isn't that what you wanted? To present a united front in public, but live private lives behind the scenes?"

He raked a bronzed hand through his black hair. "That was your invention, not mine."

"Invention—" Too shaken to talk, she got to her feet. "I...I think you'd better leave and we'll talk later when we've both had a chance to cool down."

"If you think that's going to happen, then you haven't got a clue about me."

She had every intention of going to her bedroom, but he blocked the way. "We'll sort this out now." He'd closed in on her.

"Lucca—" Alex had this suffocating feeling in her chest.

He reached for her. "I love the way you say my name in that husky voice," he murmured against her lips. Then his mouth closed over hers with a hunger she would never have imagined. This wasn't like the other times. Not anything like the other times.

He clamped her hard against him, eliminating any air between them. The feel of his powerful legs against hers was so erotic they almost buckled. She clung helplessly to him.

"Kiss me back, Alexandra. I need to taste your mouth. It was agony to have to walk away from you this morning and face a crowd when it was the last thing I wanted to do."

His confession was a revelation that broke down her defenses. She found herself melting against him, giving him a response not even she was prepared for. Their kisses turned molten. Like rivers of fire they merged in an explosion of flame, consuming everything in their path. She lost track of time and surroundings.

When he finally allowed her to breathe, she was delirious with yearnings he'd brought to life, exposing her to herself. She'd never slept with a man, but she was precariously close to begging Lucca to make love to her. Once that happened she would despise herself for the same weakness that had driven her mother into so many men's arms.

"Tell me something my sweet, vulnerable Alexandra—" he nibbled her neck and throat, deepening her desire "—is your relationship with Manny this passionate? Do you give yourself so completely to him, too, when he reaches for you?"

His questions penetrated her consciousness.

Lucca was jealous!

Despite Regina's insistence, Alex hadn't believed he was capable of that emotion. Yet the way he was acting now made her wonder.

Lucca was a man and could separate his emotions. Italian men particularly were noted for having a wife who bore their children and a lover who fulfilled their fantasies. Being his fiancée, she didn't fit in either category yet, and he was sexually frustrated. As Regina had told her, Lucca was a possessive man. After he learned the truth about Manny, his ardor would cool.

Her hands slid from the back of his neck. "Lucca, Manny Horowitz is in his fifties. He's probably the most sought-after agent in Hollywood and one of the nicest.

"When my mother was eighteen, he discovered her singing in a nightclub. After pulling her out of obscurity, he built her career and stuck with her until the very end. She repaid him by still owing him two million dollars when she died. He's never asked me for one dime of it."

Lucca kneaded her shoulders while he stared into her eyes. "Until today. Is that what made you ill? Was he hoping you would ask me for the money and you were afraid to approach me? I'll send it to him right now."

No. Her head moved from side to side in a drugged-like state.

"You know I'd give it to you in an instant."

Tears stung her eyelids. "I know, but his request had nothing to do with you."

"After the news conference, you expect me to believe that?"

"Yes," she answered soberly.

"Why are you so reluctant to tell me what his phone call was all about?"

Moisture bathed her cheeks. "Because I'm tempted to do what he wants, but it would mean asking something of you that wouldn't be fair."

"Is it illegal or immoral?" He was being perfectly serious.

"Worse. Do you remember saying that ours wouldn't be an orthodox marriage?"

Lucca kissed her moist eyelids for his answer.

She couldn't handle his tenderness and moved out of his arms. "I'll be right back."

Once Alex reached the bathroom, she washed her face and freshened up. When she returned to the bedroom, she found him out on the balcony with his back toward her. After the brief rapture they'd shared where she'd all but given herself away, she approached him with trepidation.

"What if I told you there was a way for me to pay back the twelve million dollars within the year?"

He turned around, resting his hip against the railing in a totally masculine stance. Those dark, intelligent eyes looked their fill. "I take it Manny wants to turn you into an even greater film star than your mother." His gravelly voice sounded like it had escaped from a hidden grotto.

"One movie. The revenue would solve all my financial problems."

Lucca shifted his weight. "I still don't understand your dilemma."

She took a second breath. "Don't you?"

His face lost expression. "You want out of our arrangement?"

"I would never do that to you."

"You want my permission to make the movie?"

"I'm not asking for that either," she cried in anguish, "but when you compare three or four months of work to maybe ten to twelve years if not much longer for the same kind of money... Manny says the revenue will surpass anything in recent history. Just think—I could pay him and the creditors right away."

Lines marred his features. "What's the movie about?"

Alex rubbed her arms nervously. "The life of Greta Garbo."

He pursed his lips. "I can't imagine anyone more perfect than you to impersonate her, but the answer is no, Alexandra. I need a *wife,* not an actress!"

"You don't have to sound so angry about it," she fired back, wounded. "I've tried to do everything you've asked of me. Why are you being so unfair?"

His eyes narrowed. "Whatever happened to your dreams of becoming a plastic surgeon?"

"That hasn't changed. I wish—"

"You wish we hadn't met?" he finished for her. "It's too late for that." The bleakness of his tone devastated her.

"Those are your thoughts, Lucca, not mine."

"Then what are you saying?"

"I'm saying that whatever I do, it's not right for you."

"Suppose you let me be the judge of my needs."

"When you say that, it makes me feel like you're carrying the whole burden."

"You see our relationship as a burden?" came the frosty query.

"No," she cried. "Now you're twisting my words, but let's face it. I bring a lot of excess baggage to the wedding," she mumbled, fighting her chaotic emotions. "You heard that journalist ask about my father."

"You handled him beautifully."

"Only because you gave me confidence. You see, Lucca?" She eyed him directly. "You don't have *any* baggage." Except for the woman he loved. She would always have to remain unexposed.

Alex heard his sharp intake of breath. "Everyone has baggage, but I don't put your parents in that category any more than I do my own. Forget Manny's proposition and come with me."

She sniffed. "You mean, you're still in the mood?"

His sudden smile transformed him into a man five years younger. She could hardly keep up with his mercurial behavior. "When we're talking about my motorcycle, always."

Since he was making an effort, she would to. "I'd love it. Let's go."

Once they'd gone downstairs, he put her into the limo, then took off on a black-and-silver sport bike without any sign of the Vittorio royal crest. In his leathers and black helmet, no one would guess he was the prince.

Good luck to his bodyguards trying to keep up with him.

The chauffeur drove Alex to a motorcycle dealership where they outfitted her with her own helmet and boots.

While she was trying on a leather jacket, Lucca walked in, bigger than life. He checked to be sure it was the right size. After tossing her a pair of gloves, they left through the rear door.

Lucca got on the cycle first. "This is the best part, Alexandra. All day I've been waiting to feel those fabulous legs of yours tucked around mine." Heat filled her cheeks. "Climb on and hold me tight around the waist. We're going for a ride to Eze."

"Eze?"

"When we get there, you won't need an explanation."

He told her how to get on and made certain she was comfortable.

"Ready?"

She gave the thumb's-up signal.

Down went his face mask. He revved the motor and wound his way through a couple of back streets to the main road. Progress was slow. She feared he was driving this way on purpose not to frighten her. But that's what she got for thinking, because the second they reached the coast highway he opened her up and let it rip.

There ought to be a better word than *ecstasy,* but she couldn't think of one. All she could do was cling to his leather-clad torso and let him do all the work. He drove like a pro racer, weaving in and out of traffic with precision. She had a legitimate excuse to press against his strong back and relished the sensation.

They whizzed by a sign for Ventimiglia. Soon the signs were written in French. They passed through Menton and came to Monaco. Then they began the climb up the Moyenne Corniche road. Alex had seen films portraying this area between Monte Carlo and Nice, but nothing took the place of being here in person, clutching Lucca as if her life depended on it. The realization came to Alex he *was* her whole life.

She saw the sign for Eze before they reached it. The medieval village sat perched like an eagle's nest on a rocky peak overlooking the Mediterranean. But unlike the tiny hamlet of "crag," this spot was offset by a multitude of souvenir shops and streets full of tourists.

Lucca pulled to the side of the road across the road from a shop and shut off the motor. She jumped down first and removed her helmet. He followed suit, his eyes never straying from her face. "What do you think?"

Alex studied him briefly. With his hair disheveled from the helmet, she thought him the most exciting man in existence. "I think riding with you is going to become my addiction."

Something flickered in the darkest recesses of his eyes. "I'm pleased to hear it. What about the view?"

What view? Being with Lucca blotted out everything else from her consciousness.

CHAPTER EIGHT

Lucca was still trying to recover from that moment of ecstasy in her arms and the period of agony that followed.

"Well, what do you think?" he queried again just to say something to break the silence.

"It's stupendous, but then, so is the one from Dirupo where civilization hasn't encroached. Did I pronounce *Dirupo* right?" Alex answered breathlessly.

"Perfettamente."

"I'm serious."

"So am I. There was no trace of an American accent just then."

"Thank you. With only one word to pronounce, there shouldn't be." She rolled her eyes, an unconscious trait he never tired of watching. "Wait until I try to string a sentence together. But I'll keep working on it, Lucca, for you."

"You sound charming."

"Americans don't sound charming. Ours isn't a charming language."

A smile lifted the corner of his mouth. "Who told you that?"

"No one. You can simply tell. The way you speak Italian, Lucca, it sounds beautiful, like melted butter dripping all over the place. Americans speak English like they're spewing meat through a grinder, plopping big globs everywhere."

Lucca thought he'd heard everything, but that wasn't the case because he never knew what was going to come out of that succulent mouth. Earlier it had given him a heart attack. Right now he couldn't stop laughing.

"You see?" She grinned. "I was right."

He held up his hands. "As they say in your country, I plead the Fifth."

"Always the diplomat, and brilliant besides," she muttered.

Once his shoulders stopped shaking he said, "Are you hungry?"

"Yes! You didn't know your grocery bill was going to go up when you took me on."

He chuckled once more. "It's worth the price for the pleasure of your entertaining company. Let's go inside the *epicerie* across the road. You choose the items for our picnic."

"And what will you do?"

"Hold the basket for you."

After he took both their helmets and locked them on his bike, he slid his hand up her back to her tender neck and guided her toward the store. In the open doorway was an inviting display of fruits and vegetables.

All the little signs were in French, but she'd learned her first Italian lesson on foods well enough to impress him. "We'll have *pane, mela, formaggio* and *suco d'uva.*" She dropped the items in the basket. Darting him an impish glance she said, "Can we afford dessert?"

"What do you have your eye on?"

"Anything. You choose."

"Done." He took two napoleons from the plate and put

them in the basket. They moved to the counter so he could pay. It had been too long since Lucca had enjoyed this kind of fun with a woman.

As he was putting his wallet back in his jeans his cell phone rang. It was Carlo. *"Si?"*

"Someone broke through the blockade and rammed into your cycle!"

"Accidenti!"

Alexandra knew that word well enough and shot him an anxious glance. He turned away from her.

"We don't know if it was intentional. Leave through the back door where the limo's waiting to drive you to the helicopter."

"Capisco." He hung up.

"Lucca?"

"No time for explanations now. Come with me."

Paolo was there to help hustle her through the back of the shop to the alley. A dozen of Lucca's people hovered around three limos. Now that he had Alexandra to worry about, he was thankful for the added security.

"What's wrong?" she begged after they drove away.

"Some crazy ran into the motorcycle."

"Oh, no—"

"It might have been accidental. Whatever the explanation, I'm not taking any chances with you."

Another minute and they arrived at the helipad where he helped her into the helicopter. Within seconds it lifted off and he could relax.

"Sorry about our picnic, *bellissima.* Another time."

"Do you think I care?" she cried softly. "What if someone was intentionally trying to hurt you?"

"It's happened before."

She shuddered. "I'll never complain about Carlo and Paolo again." Her eyes searched his. "This will be all over the news. What will you father say when he finds out? It could set him back."

"By now he's already been told you and I escaped any injury," Lucca muttered morosely. "Until the coronation, we'll maintain a low profile. That'll keep both him and my mother happy."

"Lucca?" He could hear her mind working. "Do you always plan exactly where you're going to be at any given moment?"

He clasped the hand closest to him. "Pretty much."

"That kind of kills any spontaneity on your part."

"*Si.*"

"It must be hard on your security people, too."

"I'm afraid there'll be times when it'll be much harder on you."

"Forget me."

Then he might as well quit breathing. "We're almost home. I'm afraid I'm going to be tied up for a while with the debriefing. Do me a favor and relax. I'll have dinner sent up to your room. Feel free to explore any part of the palace you like. If it's possible, I'll join you later."

"That won't be necessary. I'm going to work on my next lesson and impress you."

If she did any more to impress him, he was seriously thinking of a honeymoon before the ceremony.

Besides today's incident, which brought home as nothing else could the fact that Alexandra's life had been in danger, he needed to get his security people to do a thorough background check on Manny Horowitz. Lucca wanted to know chapter and verse about the man preying on Alex. The phone call from her mother's agent was the one contingency he hadn't conceived of when contemplating the many obstacles to their marriage.

He didn't really believe she had a romantic interest in Manny, but he didn't want her going near the man no matter the reason. The desire to pay off her mother's debts had driven her to fall in with Lucca's plans, but even he could see how Manny's offer held great appeal. A love of acting could be in her blood and she just didn't know it yet. Alexandra was a Carlisle after all, still young and damnably vulnerable.

The woman journalist had been right. Alexandra could have any man she wanted. Some idiot actor could get to her. There'd be physical intimacy on the set with the men playing opposite her. She could be enticed to do another picture and another. It would be an escape from the prison she'd walked into by agreeing to marry him. One day she'd want her freedom and reach for it without looking back.

That wasn't the way Lucca intended for things to happen. That wasn't acceptable. *"Maledizzione!"*

He felt a light touch on his arm. "Lucca? Does that mean damn or hell?"

Alexandra, Alexandra.

Regina rushed down the steps to embrace them. She cried something in Italian to Lucca before remembering to speak English.

"Are you all right?" she asked Alex, her eyes full of concern.

Before Alex could answer, Lucca pressed a hard kiss to her mouth. "I'll see you later," he whispered. After tweaking Regina's cheek he took the steps two at a time to the second floor.

His physical demonstrations of love for the benefit of the family were getting more difficult for Alex to handle when she knew the real reason behind them. Trying to ward off the latest assault on her senses, she linked her arm through Regina's and they finished climbing the stairs to the second floor. Both of them watched his swift progress down the hall toward their parents' suite.

"Thank God nothing happened to you." Regina sounded shaken. Slowly they moved in the direction of their own bedrooms.

"I had no idea anything was going on. We were in a small grocery store and suddenly Lucca told me we had to leave."

"Then you don't know?" his sister cried.

"About the motorcycle, yes."

"No." She shook her head. "The police uncovered a plot to assassinate Lucca. It won't have been the first time. He had a close call in Rio a year ago while he was there doing business."

"How close?"

"He was shot."

Alex gasped.

"Carlo was able to deflect the bullet. It lodged in Lucca's shoulder instead of his heart."

She squeezed her eyes together. For a moment Alex felt sick to her stomach. Lucca had been so clever in playing down the trouble today, she had no clue of the magnitude of the situation.

"He's all right, Alexandra. So far four men have been arrested, one of them a plant at the motorcycle dealership Lucca patronizes."

"We were just there," her voice trailed shakily.

Regina nodded. "Intelligence says two more men are

involved but have left the country. It's because they don't want Lucca on the throne. Since Papa's illness last year, Lucca has virtually run the government. His rigid policy for closed immigration borders and strict banking laws has frustrated certain elements as you can imagine."

"Do you agree with him?"

"Absolutely. Papa has stopped short of allowing electronic eavesdropping for surveillance to go on, but once Lucca is king, all that is going to change and the enemy knows it."

Alex shuddered. "He'll never be safe, will he?"

"No, but his first duty is to keep the rest of us safe."

Regina sounded like a queen herself.

"That explains why there was so much extra security at the House of Savoy in New York."

Her dark head whipped around. "So that was the shop you referred to at the press conference? I've been dying to know where your great love affair began."

Alex moaned inwardly. "He was in the security room with his bodyguards and saw me on one of the monitors getting upset with the head jeweler."

"My brother can't make a move without a small army protecting him."

The reason Lucca hadn't been to see his lover was no longer a mystery. It looked like it was time for Regina to know everything. Until his sister was armed with the whole truth about the reason for their engagement, Alex wouldn't be able to help him.

"Regina? Will you have dinner with me in my room?"

"I was going to suggest we eat together. Mama and Papa want to be alone with Lucca."

"I'm sure he wants that, too, if only to reassure them he won't be planning any more crazy outings with me."

"They're not crazy." His sister sounded mournful. "He just wants to live a normal life like other men."

Alex opened the door to her suite. "There's something else he wants, Regina."

"What do you mean?"

The way she asked that question in all naiveté led Alex to believe Lucca's sister really didn't know about his secret love.

He was a private man who gave so little away, you had to have radar to catch the slips. Alex had a private nature, too. Maybe that was why she'd been able to pick up on them.

"Come inside and let's talk."

Once they'd ordered a sandwich, Alex took off her new leather jacket and boots and curled up on one end of the couch. Regina slipped out of her sandals and tucked her legs beneath her on the chair facing Alex.

"Regina…what I'm going to tell you has to stay between us."

She crossed herself. "I swear it."

Alex sat forward. "You're going to fight me on it."

Lucca's sister looked utterly bewildered. After a long pause she said, "I promise I won't."

"Grazie." Both women smiled at each other with a perfect understanding.

"Your brother's in love."

"I know. He's so madly in love with you, I'm euphoric. So are my parents. None of us thought it would or could happen. When he asked me to meet him at the plane, I knew he'd reached the darkest point in his life and needed me. I'm afraid that's why I fell apart the moment I saw him. I was so upset for him, I didn't realize you were standing nearby."

"He's a better actor than my mother ever was."

Alex waited for those words to sink in before she continued.

"There's a commoner he's been in love with for a long time. I don't know her name. We don't discuss her. I have no idea if she's Castelmarian, French, Italian, British, Australian or American, or from somewhere else entirely for that matter. I'm presuming they spend their time together whenever he leaves the country to go on those six-week business trips."

Regina stayed true to her word. She didn't make a sound, but suddenly her lovely face was all brown eyes.

"If she *is* one of your countrywomen, then the heightened security would explain why he hasn't tried to be with her since our arrival. However, I'm digressing from the main point which is this—your brother and I are getting married to solve two problems that appeared insoluble to us both until we met. Love doesn't come into it and never did."

Alex waited for lightning to strike her dead. When it didn't, she unloaded on poor Regina who sat there for the next five minutes looking shell-shocked. "So now you understand everything."

The words had scarcely left her mouth when the maid knocked and brought in a tray. After thanking her and seeing her to the door, Alex walked back to Regina.

"What I need you to do is go to him in private and tell him that you know the truth. Convince him I want to help him so he can be with her before the wedding. She needs an explanation.

"He'll be furious with me, but I don't care. His happiness and safety are more important to me than anything else in this world." Her voice trembled. "I know you feel the same way. On the plane I witnessed that love."

Regina's eyes filled, but she continued to remain silent.

"I have a plan." One that had been burning up Alex's mind during the motorcycle ride to Eze. The scare after they'd been shopping for a picnic had set the seal on it. "Tell Lucca it will enable him to be with her right away without worrying about anyone's safety.

"When he asks why I didn't talk to him about this myself, tell him I didn't think he would take me seriously. But I knew he'd listen to you because he loves and trusts you, Regina. We both need your support if this is going to work."

Alex took another fortifying breath. "You, above all people, know how much he's suffered over the years knowing he would have to marry someone he didn't love. It shouldn't have to happen to anyone. My mother went in and out of six marriages. None of them worked, and her life was a ruin.

"I don't want that for Lucca. He's the most unselfish, wonderful man in the world and deserves every happiness. With your backing we can help make his life bearable. Will you do it?" she implored.

Regina's solemn eyes stared at her for the longest time. "How could I not? What's your plan?"

Lucca bade the head of security good-night. It was close to midnight. Much as he wanted to talk to Alexandra, he would have to wait until tomorrow. She'd be asleep by now. Though he was exhausted, it was the emotional kind. He was positive he wouldn't be able to sleep yet and opted to go for a swim in the pool in front of the palace.

He slipped out the south entrance into the warm night air and ambled down the steps. After leaving his T-shirt and jeans in a pile, he removed his socks and boots. For the sake of propriety because he was never solely alone, he kept on his boxers and dove into the tepid water.

On his tenth lap he heard a splash. Was it Alexandra?

His heart practically leaped out of his chest until he realized it was his sister doing the breaststroke toward him, leaving him fiercely disappointed.

Lucca's sister was a champion swimmer. Still, he couldn't help but wonder what had brought her out here this time of night.

"*Ao, piccina.*"

"*Ciao, fratello mio.* I've been waiting to talk to you. This is the perfect spot." They both treaded water.

"You sound serious tonight."

"I am."

Some nuance in her voice convinced him. "Did the parents send you?"

"No."

"I give up. What's on your mind?"

"Alexandra has told me everything."

"Everything covers a lot of territory," he teased, not liking the direction this conversation had taken.

"Please let me talk until I'm finished. This time I won't let you put me off because you're uncomfortable."

He tossed his head back to stop the water from dripping in his eyes. "Is that what I do?"

"When it gets too personal, yes, it's exactly what you do. Like you're doing right now."

"Consider me suitably chastened."

"Lucca…I know the real reason why Alexandra is going to marry you. While you fund her tuition for medical school, she'll play the loving fiancée to get you off the hook. She told me all about the fake diamonds and her mother's debts. I understand she plans to pay them off by earning the money. It does her great credit."

"I agree."

"What I don't understand is why you told her you were in love with someone else when we both know it's not true?"

"That's my business."

"Not any longer, but I'm beginning to understand why she asked for my help. You can be forbidding over the things you hold most dear. Did you know she has an elaborate plan to help you and your supposed lover spend some time together before the wedding without putting you at risk? I think it's the most selfless thing I ever heard of."

"Go on." He couldn't wait to hear the rest. Alexandra's mind fascinated him.

"She has to fly to Los Angeles to finish closing up her apartment."

A tight band constricted his breathing. "How is that supposed to aid me?" It seemed his fiancée had conveniently left Manny out of the conversation with his sister.

No way was Lucca going to let her go near him, not since his security people had found out the agent had a lot more to do with her mother's bankruptcy than anyone had let on. He'd been taking huge cuts out of her income for years and figured he could do the same with Alexandra. Lucca would protect her from that barracuda at all costs.

"She'll be coming right back, Lucca. When she returns to Castelmare, she intends to bring a friend with her for the upcoming wedding. That friend will be your fictional lover."

"For once I have to confess I'm speechless."

"You haven't heard anything yet! Alexandra's done makeup for years and says that if you're worried about anyone recognizing your girlfriend, she can change her looks enough so that no one could identify her. I'd say it was a master plan. She even thinks they'll stay in the blue suite together where you can have access to her."

Santo Cielo!

Only Alexandra could have concocted anything so diabolically clever and insane at the same time. Today's assassination attempt had brought out that deep well of compassion inside her. In the process she'd inveigled his tender-hearted sister, who'd worried over his secret sadness for too many years.

He moved to the edge of the pool and levered himself up onto the deck. Regina climbed out behind him. "You can't let this lie go on any longer. She deserves the truth. Why have you allowed her to go on believing something so outrageous?"

"I have my reasons." Lucca was still waiting for Sofia to return his call and release him from the promise he'd made to keep her plans a secret. The newscast announcing his forthcoming marriage to Alexandra had already devastated Sofia's parents. There'd been phone calls to his parents. The sooner Sofia explained everything to her parents, the sooner the pain, for everyone, could end.

"Don't take too long to be honest with her. She wants to leave for Los Angeles right away."

He pulled on his jeans. After he'd gathered his other clothes, they returned to the palace. When they reached the second floor, he said, "I'll talk to her tomorrow afternoon."

"Why don't you tell her first thing in the morning?"

"Because Papa has to go into the hospital for blood work and Mama wants me there. I'll be back in time to give Alexandra another Italian lesson."

"What do you mean another?"

"Until Professor Emilio returns, I've decided to take a break from my work schedule to give her some of my time each afternoon."

In the privacy of the schoolroom he would tell her about Manny, who'd used her mother mercilessly. Lucca would do anything to protect her. He hoped this new information would help her develop a more-positive view of her parent.

Regina eyed him speculatively. "Are you sure you want to do that?"

"You don't approve?"

"Of course, but cut her a little slack. Not everyone is the scary perfectionist you are. I ought to know. *Buonanotte.*"

Alex left for the schoolroom in a nervous state. She thought by now she would have heard from Lucca. A phone call. Anything. But he'd been out of touch. So had Regina, who, Alex had found out the day before, volunteered at an animal shelter run by her family.

The local news channel had been showing repeated clips of the smashed motorcycle followed by photos of the men arrested. She could follow bits and pieces of the Italian coverage because she'd been part of the story.

Though there were no clips of her and Lucca on his sport bike, they replayed segments from the broadcast showing him kissing the back of her hand. The television audience could be forgiven for thinking the crown prince was truly in love.

Had his lover seen the coverage? How could she stand to know he might have been killed yesterday? How could she bear to see him with Alex?

"Buon pomeriggio, Alexandra."

Her heart did a kick. *"Buon pomeriggio, Lucca."*

She didn't quite know what to expect this afternoon. If Regina had found an opportunity to talk to him already, then there was no telling how angry he was that his sister had learned the truth behind their engagement. Even if he adored Regina, he would consider that Alex had broken a sacred trust.

Right now she couldn't gauge his frame of mind. Being a royal he'd learned how to present a facade that gave nothing away.

Today he'd dispensed with a suit in favor of chinos and a dark green pullover. He always smelled wonderful. Afraid to be caught staring, she quickly averted her eyes and opened up her notebook to the exercises she'd written out.

He walked by her desk and reached for it. His arm brushed against her shoulder, reminding her of the way he'd made her feel when he'd crushed her against his hard body yesterday. She was a fool to expect a repeat performance, but the sensual part of her nature ached to experience those sensations again.

Until Lucca had aroused her passion, she'd thought she was one of those women who couldn't get worked up over a man, probably because of her mother's pattern of going from one unsatisfying relationship to another. Yet all he'd had to do was pluck her from the Grigory royal tree—yes, plucked—and after he'd taken one bite, she'd practically begged to be devoured whole.

"No mistakes," he muttered. "*Molto bene.* Now let's see how you do with your second verb. The most important one after 'to be,'" he added in a tone as smooth as satin.

"To eat?" she quipped, knowing full well he'd meant something else.

"*Mangiare* comes third." He sat on the corner of the

teacher's desk, way too close to her. "Repeat after me." His dark eyes impaled her. *"Io amo."*

Alex struggled to maintain her composure. *"Io amo."* I love you, her heart whispered. Could he hear it?

"Again."

She looked down at her book, unable to sustain his glance. *"Io amo."*

"Perfetto," he declared. *"Tu ami."*

The lesson continued until she'd gone through all the conjugations of *amare*.

"Eccellente. You've mastered the present tense of the three verbs necessary for happiness."

"Only three?"

He crossed his powerful legs at the ankles. "To be alive, to love, to eat— What else is required?"

Maybe this was his way of letting her know Regina had talked to him. Alex had to risk finding out.

"For everyone else, nothing more. For the king, an added subtlety—to be able to love the woman he wants?" she challenged, meeting his gaze head-on.

His expression remained inscrutable. "So you think we need to add a fourth verb to the list of life's necessities?" The air thickened with tension.

"Where the king is concerned, yes."

A lengthy silence ensued. "As long as you felt compelled to tell Regina the truth, why didn't you reveal all of it?"

The question he shot at her was one she wasn't prepared for. Her gentle frown gave her a piquant look. "What do you mean?"

Lucca stood up. "What about Manny and his film offer? I told you before I didn't want you to do it, but I'm afraid now it's out of the question. I had him investigated. He not only exploited your mother, he milked her out of millions of dollars and should be brought up on criminal charges."

She lowered her head. "I think I already figured that out. My mother must have been the perfect pawn. This morning I phoned him and told him I wasn't interested in his offer."

Lucca's solid body froze in place. "And he accepted it, just like that?"

"He had no choice. I told him I'm getting married and want as far away from Hollywood as possible for the rest of my life."

Grazie a Dio.

She chewed on her lower lip. "I hope you don't mind that I won't be able to pay you back for my schooling for a long time."

He moved closer to her. "We've already had that discussion. Let me pay the twelve million dollars and be done with it."

"No, Lucca. We made a pact."

He hadn't meant to put more pressure on her. "So we did. What I want to know is why you told Regina you were flying to Los Angeles. We've already dealt with your apartment and personal things."

Her gaze collided with his. "Didn't she tell you about my plan to get you and your lover together?"

His hands gripped her shoulders. For a minute Lucca *had* forgotten. The knowledge that she'd turned Manny down flat had driven everything else from his mind.

"As my sister said, it was a selfless thought on your part, Alexandra, but it would never have worked."

"You're right," she muttered. "I should have realized it would never have worked. I've been thinking what I could

REBECCA WINTERS   155

do to help the two of you, but sneaking her into the palace under false pretenses is pretty absurd.

"The thing is, yesterday it hit me hard that you're a prisoner in so many dreadful ways. How can you possibly be with her when your every move is under surveillance? I...I thought I could help," she stammered.

Lucca needed to be released from his promise to Sofia ASAP. He relinquished his hold on her before he lost complete control. "You'll never know what your concern means to me, Alexandra. Give me a little more time and I'll tell you all about her."

She nodded. "Please forgive me for involving Regina. The poor thing. I was terrible to her," she admitted.

He eyed her speculatively. "In what way?"

"I asked her to listen to me and not interrupt because I knew she would fight me. Regina loves you so much, she did exactly as I said. I've never met a sweeter person. She knew it was futile to go to you, but she did it for me."

"My sister cares a great deal for you."

She moistened her lips anxiously. "But you're angry with me for telling her."

"You're wrong, Alexandra. I've taken you away from everything familiar. When I swore you to secrecy, I hadn't considered how much you would need a friend to confide in."

She peeked at him from beneath her lashes. "Who is it you confide in?"

Before Alexandra had come into his life, he and Sofia had used each other to commiserate, but those days were over. "I have *you* now."

"That places a grave responsibility on me," she whispered.

He studied her for a moment. "When I asked you to

marry me, you didn't realize what you were getting into. I'm afraid I didn't play fair."

Alex brushed an errant curl from her forehead. "You've been more than fair. Thank you for finding out about Manny. I've been naive about so many things, but I'm learning."

"Aren't we all," he whispered. "Can I hope you don't hate me too much?"

"That question doesn't deserve an answer." Alex let out a tormented sigh. "I haven't even asked about your parents. How's your father? When I watched the news this morning, all I could think of was his reaction."

He rubbed the back of his bronzed neck absently. "Now that I've promised him there'll be no unnecessary trips outside the palace until the honeymoon, he was in surprisingly good spirits after his blood test this morning and hasn't had to rely on his oxygen today."

"I'm glad he's doing that well." She hugged her arms to her chest. "I guess we have to take a honeymoon."

He nodded. "Where would you like to go, and I'll get my security people working on it."

Her pulse quickened. "I haven't traveled much, so anything would sound exciting. Is there some place you've never been you'd like to visit?"

"Dozens of them."

Every once in a while she heard that yearning in his voice to disappear to the other side of the planet and be accountable to no one.

"What would be the easiest as far as security's concerned?"

"The yacht."

"I've never been on one."

"It's ideal if you're looking for relaxation."

She cast him a worried glance. "Would that appeal to you?"

"I have to admit it would be for the best. As long as we're somewhere on the Mediterranean, it's not too far away should Papa take a turn for the worse."

"Then it's settled. I'll have hours every day to practice my Italian. What will you do?"

"Besides teach you?" A ghost of a smile hovered around his mouth. "Probably get back to my research."

"What kind?"

"I'm a geophysicist."

"You are?" Alex was stunned. She blinked. "So if you didn't have to be king—"

"I would go on doing fieldwork around the globe looking for new diamond finds to shore up more resources for Castelmare."

Her hand automatically crept to the pin attached to her cotton knit top. His gaze settled on it. "The Ligurian diamond is the reason I became interested in the subject. To understand how they're formed and where to look for them captivated me from the outset."

"I knew there was something more significant about this stone than the obvious."

His eyes lifted to hers. "It has been my lucky piece in more ways than one."

"How so?" she whispered. His nearness made her feel giddy.

"It brought me to New York at the precise moment Kathryn Carlisle's daughter walked through the doors. Call it destiny... Kismet...our meeting lifted me out of the black void of my existence. For agreeing to marry me, you have my eternal devotion."

Devotion, not love, so don't kill me with your earthshaking brand of kindness, Lucca.

Her plea came too late as he cupped her face in his hands and lowered his mouth to hers. It wasn't like yesterday after his escape from harm when he'd taken out his desires on her because he was missing his beloved. This time he kissed her as if she were his most cherished possession.

But it couldn't go on. She wouldn't allow it, because Alex had very recently discovered she wasn't a half-a-loaf girl.

Slowly he put her from him. It wasn't a moment too soon, because in another second she would have given in to the needs engulfing her.

His gaze found hers. "We'll finish your Italian lesson tomorrow. Right now the dressmaker is with Mama. They want to go over the design for your wedding gown. Afterward we'll have dinner with the family and Regina will join us. Later my father's personal assistant will walk us through the wedding day so we won't be apprehensive."

"What do you mean 'we'?"

She heard him inhale deeply. "In case you've forgotten, I've never been married before, either. *I* could trip on the steps outside the cathedral."

"Lucca—"

He kissed the corner of her mouth. Alex felt it long after they'd left the schoolroom.

CHAPTER NINE

FOR the next two weeks a routine was established. Mostly Alex saw Lucca when he came upstairs to help her with her Italian. Afterward they usually had dinner with his parents. When she wasn't studying, she often swam with Regina in the indoor pool and worked out in the palace gym.

Three days before the wedding, Professor Emilio made his appearance in the schoolroom. She put on a happy face, but inside she was wretchedly disappointed that her formal lessons with Lucca had come to an end.

The professor was a fine teacher and complimented her on her progress so far. She had no complaints. It was just that those two hours alone with Lucca had become the focal point of her daily existence.

Now that he was sequestered in his office dealing with government business and finishing his coronation speech, she hardly saw him. If this was setting a precedent for the future, then she needed to stop feeling sorry for herself and get on with plans that didn't include Lucca.

After breakfast she phoned Regina and asked if she'd go to the university with her. It was time for her to look into taking the exam that would allow her to go to medical school. She could study for it on her honeymoon. Regina fell in with her plans at once. They decided to make a full day of it, with lunch and shopping thrown in.

At five that afternoon Alex heard a man call to her. She and Regina were about to leave the university's student test center. She turned to her left.

"Tomaso! Come va?"

He seemed to have materialized out of nowhere. His dark blue eyes were alive with obvious pleasure. *"In questo momento sono di ottimo umore. E tu?"*

That was one of the greetings she'd practiced with Lucca. Tomaso had just said he was in a good mood now. It was exciting to be able to understand basic phrases.

"Molto bene."

She felt Regina nudge her arm. *"Buon pomeriggio, Professore Morelli."*

His gaze swerved to Regina. He looked taken back to see her standing there. Remembering his manners, he gave a slight bow. *"Principessa.* I'm finished for the day. May I take you ladies across the piazza for some *gelato?"*

"We'd enjoy that," Regina spoke up before Alex had the chance to turn him down. At first she didn't understand Lucca's sister until it dawned on her Regina might be attracted to the Italian professor. He *was* attractive, and intelligent.

The crowded street made their progress slow but they finally arrived at one of the little sidewalk cafés. Tomaso challenged Alex to order in Italian, then complimented her on not making one mistake. While she basked in his praise, the waiter brought them ice cream. Tomaso insisted on paying.

She'd almost finished hers when a black limo from the palace pulled up in front of the café. Regina gave Alex the eye, signaling it was time to go.

Alex ate the last spoonful before thanking Tomaso.

"Next time it will be our treat," Regina assured him.

"I'll remember." He walked them to the car. *"A presto,"* he said after they were settled.

When the door closed, Regina smiled at her. "I think you're in trouble."

"Why?"

"I didn't arrange for this limo. It means one of your bodyguards phoned Lucca."

"We didn't do anything wrong."

"That doesn't matter. My brother won't care that I was the one who accepted Professor Morelli's invitation."

"Lucca told me my bodyguards would never say anything unless I was in danger."

Her brows lifted. "There's danger, and then there's danger. You know what I mean?"

"But that's ridiculous."

"Tomaso is clearly infatuated with you," Regina declared.

There was little point in arguing with her, because Alex had to admit he'd acted a little too happy to see her.

"Why did you accept his invitation, Regina?"

"Because my brother dismissed him too fast for something that wasn't his fault. I wanted to let him know it wasn't anything personal."

"I think that was wonderful of you." She smiled. "If Lucca says anything, I'll defend you to the death."

"Let's hope it doesn't come to that."

"Regina—"

She opened her smoke tinted window a crack. "Don't look now, but there he is."

"Who?"

"Lucca. I can tell from here he's in battle mode."

Alex's husband-to-be made a frightening adversary

when provoked, but this time she had right on her side and would stand up to him. However, when he opened the rear door, her heartbeat tripled at the breathtaking sight of him, knocking her off balance. He was dressed in cream trousers and a black silk shirt, exuding a male potency to die for. Before she could recover, he leaned inside.

"Welcome home, *amata*," he murmured against her lips. "Umm. You taste of strawberry gelato. That was very nice of Professor Morelli." His gaze made an intimate appraisal, taking in her light blue two-piece suit, another outfit he'd asked her to try on at the shop.

"About him, Lucca, he—"

"We'll talk about it later," he broke in. "Your uncle Yuri arrived an hour ago and is eager to see you."

The palace had been filling up with Lucca's closest relatives, all of whom were gracious, but none of them were her family. Warmth filled her system to realize her own great-uncle had come. "I can't wait to see him."

Compassion shone from Lucca's eyes as he helped her from the limo. "He brought more of your father's family with him. Right now he's with Papa. I'll take you up there."

Alex saw no sign of Regina, who'd disappeared without her realizing it. She must have taken their things with her, including a brochure and several handouts from the university.

They started up the stairs with his hand in its usual place at the back of her neck. While he asked her how soon she could take the test, she felt his fingers rub her skin with disturbing insistence.

"When e-ever I feel ready." The answer came out jerkily. "They'll let me do it in English, but after that—" It was impossible to concentrate with him touching her. Lucca had no idea at all how impossible it was to be around him anymore and pretend she wasn't affected by the little things he did.

He was a sensual man. To her shock she'd discovered that she was a sensual creature, too. Every move he made, whether it was the way he sometimes made furrows in his hair without realizing it, or slipped off his jacket to get comfortable before they started a lesson. Whatever he did was guaranteed to draw her attention, filling her mind with forbidden thoughts that caused her to blush.

She wanted to run her hands through his hair. She dreamed of removing his jacket and tie and shirt so she could really touch him. She desired so many things she couldn't have. When Lucca had once asked her to join him swimming, she'd purposely avoided it. He'd never pressed her, but it was a pleasure she knew he enjoyed.

If she gave in to the temptation, he would know she wasn't in control. Then it would all come out that she was a fraud, that she'd clearly and simply fallen in love with him in Mr. Defore's office and would have followed him to the ends of the earth if he'd asked it of her.

"That's quite a conversation you're having with yourself," he whispered against her cheek. They'd reached the entrance to his parents' suite and she hadn't even noticed.

"I just wanted you to know that it was by chance Regina and I met Professor Morelli."

Maybe he didn't realize it, but he'd backed her up against one of the doors with his arms loosely holding her. "I'm quite aware he did all the running. As I told you before, it'll happen over and over again in your life because you're a beautiful woman who's totally unaware of her appeal. That's what makes you a magnet for men who are free to look but know they can't touch."

Lucca might not want her, but she was about to become his legal consort and that made her his possession. She wore his diamond for everyone to see. How appropriate that he'd had it cut in the shape of a teardrop. A presentiment of things to come even at the young age of nineteen, because he knew he'd never find fulfillment in marriage? Certainly her heart was bleeding all over the place, too. A fine wedding couple they made.

Maybe now was the time to give him something she'd bought him today. He might not be her possession, but being his wife she would have certain claims on him. As king he would wear the monarch seal on his right hand. As husband, he could wear her gift on his left for everyone to see, but it wouldn't prevent the woman he loved from touching him.

"Close your eyes for a minute, Lucca."

His black brows furrowed. Whatever he'd expected her to say, that wasn't it. "Why?"

"Because I have something for you. I hope you're going to like it. I'd planned to put it on you before you left for your coronation, but I've changed my mind."

Surprise registered in his eyes before he closed them. It meant her bodyguards hadn't blabbed all to him. She would remember to thank them later.

Compared to the worth of the Ligurian diamond, the $150 she'd paid for it was negligible. She'd put the tiny box in her suit jacket pocket to wrap later.

"Remember the day you took me to Dirupo? There was a little plaque outside the church in memory of St. Anthony of Padua and his companion Lucca Belludi, a nobleman who'd traveled with him to that spot. I did a little research and learned that after St. Anthony's death, Lucca took his place, becoming the guardian and miracle worker.

"That's how I think of you, taking your father's place, becoming the guardian of the kingdom and working miracles for Castelmare."

She took the gold ring from the box and slid it on his ring finger. Regina had helped her gauge the size. It looked like a perfect fit. The face of the ring was square shaped. An outline of the head of Lucca Belludi stood out in gold against a brilliant red background of pyrope. She loved the color. It reminded her of the red in the flag of the House of Savoy.

"You can open your eyes now."

His heart nearly failed him when he looked down at the ring. While he'd been thinking up ways to pulverize Tomaso and incarcerate Manny, she'd been buying him a wedding ring unlike any other.

Lucca would never forget that day at Dirupo. There'd been so much he'd wanted to share with her he hadn't known where to start first. In the process he hadn't realized she'd paid that much attention. What she'd just told him astounded him.

This gift held a significance beyond price, but shame consumed him because he hadn't told her about Sofia yet.

How ironic that throughout his adult life he'd grieved for the kind of love he would never know, yet now that Alexandra had colored his world, he would go on grieving because it seemed the only love she felt for him translated into lofty tributes.

She'd put him on a pedestal where he didn't belong, not realizing he wanted to be in her bed, in her arms. He wanted to fill every centimeter of her heart, share every part of her soul.

So help him, if it took the rest of his life, he'd find a way. But he would have to be clever. The old tale about the sun and the wind came to mind:

The sun and the wind made a wager to see who could get the man below them to take off his coat. The wind boasted he would blow it off him, but it only resulted in the man wrapping it tighter around him. The sun smiled and kept shining until it grew so hot the man finally removed it.

That would be his technique. Just keep pouring on a little more heat until she opened up to him because she couldn't help herself.

He reached for her hands, kissing the inside of her wrists. "You've paid me a supreme compliment. I'm not worthy of it, but I'll make you a promise never to remove it. This ring will be a constant reminder of your faith in me and my great fortune in taking you for my bride. I'm the luckiest of men."

"No, you're not," she whispered in a mournful tone. "It should be the woman you love giving you the wedding gift from her heart."

Lucca couldn't take much more. "I'd rather talk about your happiness."

She avoided his eyes. "I'm very happy. To be able to go to medical school and help people one day is more than I could ask for."

"But will it be enough?"

"Like you said, we don't know what the future has in store."

Pain shot through him as real as the bullet that could have killed him last year if it had hit the intended organ. Thanks to Carlo's heroics, Lucca only had a scar near the top of his left shoulder to remind him of his mortality.

With reluctance, he let go of her. "Alexandra, something vital came up earlier I must take care of. Do you mind if I don't go in with you?"

"Of course not."

"Your uncle and I had a good chat earlier, but I'll meet up with you both later."

"Don't worry. You're about to take on a new mantle. I understand that."

It wasn't the answer he wanted, but when she never made a fuss over his comings and goings, he had no right to complain.

"Enjoy your evening with him."

She nodded before going inside.

While she looked forward to a happy reunion with one of her only living relatives, Lucca headed for Regina's suite. He rapped on her door. They had their own signal. After doing it one more time to make certain she heard it, he walked in.

She was curled up in a chair in the sitting room, brushing her hair while she watched TV. "*Ciao, caro.* I've been expecting you."

His expression grim, he turned it off. "We have to talk."

"You stole my line."

"This is serious, *piccina.*"

"I agree. You still haven't told Alexandra the truth." She put the brush down. "I happen to know you're so in love with her your behavior is off the wall. What's going on with you?"

"It's about Sofia." In the next breath he told her everything.

"All this time I thought Sofia was hurting for you," Regina murmured. "Surely you can tell Alexandra the truth now."

"I will, but——"

"Oh, Lucca," she cried out, "you're terrified she won't forgive you! I never thought I'd live to see the day my brother was frightened of anything."

Her comment brought him to a standstill.

"Do you honestly believe you could have talked a total stranger into marrying you unless she'd wanted it with the same passion?"

"She was desperate for financial help, Regina. When she wouldn't let me give her the money, I had to come up with another plan."

His sister eyed him shrewdly. "Knowing her tragic background, you do realize Alexandra would be the last woman on earth to repeat the mistakes of her mother and go near a king or be tempted by all the trappings unless she couldn't help herself. By the way, I know all about her turning down the chance to make that film."

Lucca's head reared. "When did she tell you that?"

"Today during the flight from Nice."

"What flight?" he thundered.

"The one she insisted we take to Padua, Italy, to find you that ring you're wearing."

"No one informed me!"

"They didn't dare after I threatened them with being fired. Isn't it interesting she couldn't even wait until the ceremony to give it to you. But to get back to my other point, she said she couldn't go to Hollywood because you might need her. In case you're still blind, deaf and dumb, it's code for she couldn't bear to be away from you."

Dio mio.

"I'm the one who accepted Professor Morelli's invitation for ice cream today. Alexandra wasn't the slightest bit interested and tried to stop me, but I thought it was the least I could do after your fit of jealousy drove you to get rid of him. That was totally unlike you. However, I do understand.

"Lucca—" she sighed "—there's only one answer for

her willingness to throw herself on the pyre of public scrutiny and risk the ridicule that followed her mother around in order to be your wife."

"She's never once taken the initiative to be with me."

Regina shook her head in exasperation. "Because you told her you were in love with someone else!"

He punched his fist into his palm. "Don't you think I want to believe what you're saying?"

"For someone so brilliant, there are times when you can be positively obtuse. You would never have approached Alexandra in New York if you hadn't been halfway falling in love with her already. She had to have felt the same way. You're a scientist. Show me proof that it can only happen once on a planet and that it only happened to you."

Lucca tried to find fault with her logic. Regina got out of the chair and hugged him. "I knew you couldn't." His emotions in chaos, he hugged her back harder. It was time to confess all to Alexandra.

After kissing the top of her head, he let her go. "Do I dare ask one more favor of you?"

"That all depends."

"Tonight when Alexandra comes back to her suite, use the excuse of some wedding detail to talk to her. I need the diamond pin, but I don't want her to know why. Do whatever it takes and bring it to me without alarming her."

He could hear her brain plotting. "I've got the perfect idea."

"Thank you. Did I ever tell you you're my favorite person?"

"I used to be," she muttered, but she smiled as she said it.

Needing to be by himself, he left her room and went downstairs to his office to call Sofia. Thankfully she answered. After telling her everything, Sofia felt terrible she'd held him to their secret for so long and released him from it. They wished each other the very best and promised to keep in touch. When he hung up, he felt an enormous weight had been lifted.

Now he could get down to some business he'd left off doing after learning about Alexandra's chance meeting with Professor Morelli. Regina was right. Lucca had behaved like an ass and needed to do something about it. Maybe an invitation to the wedding.

He lounged back in his swivel chair. The more he thought about it, the more he liked the idea that Tomaso would see his beautiful student pledge her life and love to her liege. Without hesitation he rang his secretary and told him to take care of it, then he got to work.

Two hours later Regina walked in his office and put the little jewel case on his desk. "Mission accomplished."

He reached for it. "What did you tell her?"

"That the people making the wedding dress needed to arrange everything ahead of time so there'd be no fuss the morning she left for the cathedral. Naturally I explained that you had authorized it."

"*Perfetto.* How did she respond?"

"She loves it more than anything, but I think she's relieved not to have the responsibility of it for a few days. I noticed she kept touching it today as if to make sure it was still there. Every woman should have such a fear."

"Is she in her room now?"

"Yes." Regina came around his desk and pecked him on the cheek. "See you tomorrow at breakfast. It'll be our last one before you're a married man."

Lucca detected a distinct wobble in her voice. "I'm not going anywhere."

"Yes, you are. You're going to a new place to start a new life with the woman you adore. That's the way it should be."

She dashed out of his office. He would have gone after her, but he knew she wouldn't want to be caught. Up until three weeks ago he'd been where she was tonight and every night before that. Grief needed no onlookers.

He rubbed his temples, then phoned the palace jeweler. "I have the item we talked about. It'll be in your hands shortly."

Once he'd buzzed his secretary and everything was taken care of, he realized he couldn't put off talking to Alexandra any longer. He rang her room. When she answered he said, "I'm coming up now." Afraid she'd find some excuse why he shouldn't, he hung up and left his office for his bedroom. He needed to change first.

Alex gripped the phone a little tighter before she put it back on the hook. Something was wrong. He'd sounded terse. She checked her watch. It was after eleven. Normally he would wait until tomorrow to talk to her.

Somewhat anxious, she went into the bathroom to freshen up, but he was at her door before she could run the brush through her hair. Sensing his impatience, she hurried to the entry and opened it. He was dressed in black bathing trunks and a dark T-shirt, the epitome of male beauty.

She felt the full battery of those brown eyes examining her. "I need to talk to you, but not here. Put on your suit and come swimming with me."

Her pulse sped up. "You mean, the indoor pool?"

"No. The one in front of the palace."

"But I thought it was only ornamental."

"During the day it is. At night when the grounds are locked up and no one can see me, I do laps to work out. Tonight I prefer being in the open. We'll slip out through the south entrance."

Just the way he talked caused her insides to melt. Being alone with him tonight wouldn't be a good idea. She'd left her terrace doors open. The air felt as if they were in the tropics.

She put a hand to her throat. "Would you mind if we do it tomorrow night instead? I'm afraid I'm still full from dinner with Uncle Yuri."

His face closed up. "You don't have to swim if you don't want to."

Without spelling it out, he was insisting she join him. Somehow she knew she wasn't going to like what he had to say.

"Give me a minute to change."

He moved inside the sitting room while she ran in the bathroom. After donning her cherry-red bikini, she put on a cotton wrap that hit her midthigh. She exchanged her heels for sandals, then met up with him at the entry.

Beneath his black-fringed lids his gaze swept over her, missing nothing. They walked down the hallway not quite touching. Her heart pounded in her throat with alternating waves of excitement and fear.

The palace grounds were a fairyland. Combined with the lights from the yachts in the bay, it was like something out of an enchanted dream complete with her own tall, dark prince. But she'd never seen him this brooding or remote. She ached to find some semblance of the man who'd worked his magic over her for the past three weeks.

Where had the man gone she'd given the ring to earlier?

He'd acted pleased, even touched by her gift, but maybe it had been a mistake. A turnoff because he didn't want any tokens from her. It wasn't part of their pact and she'd over-stepped the bounds. Was that it?

They reached the edge of the pool, but Lucca hadn't said a word yet. That, more than anything, made her feel as though someone had just knocked the wind out of her. She stepped out of her sandals. Needing to channel her pain with something physical, she whipped off her wrap and dived in.

Alex didn't care if the excuse that she was too full made a liar out of her. This silence between them was something new. She couldn't deal with it. At the end of her first lap he caught up to her. Her intention to do a second was impeded by his hand. He caught her wrist in his strong grasp. "Stay here."

As she lifted her dripping head she saw a flash of pain in his eyes. What in heaven's name was wrong? She could be forgiven for thinking someone close to him had died.

The quiet stretched between them, causing her mind to imagine other unpalatable possibilities. Tomorrow was his last day of freedom. In thirty-six hours they'd be married. Had it suddenly caught up with him that he couldn't go through with this? Was that what he needed to tell her?

She was supposed to be the one who'd decided that this was all too much. Any other woman with a modicum of pride would have fled a bogus engagement long before now. But not Alex Carlisle Grigory who'd willingly been swept off her feet into an arranged marriage.

It wasn't his fault he'd grown on her second by second from the moment they'd met until she couldn't draw another breath without him.

Alex slowly eased her arm out of his grasp. Any other

time his touch would have turned her insides to mush. Not tonight. He was in the throes of unutterable pain and her body sensed it. She had the sick feeling that at this moment the very sight of her repulsed him.

His hardened features had taken on a sculpted appearance, as if he'd been cast in bronze.

"Obviously, you're in hell, Lucca. Say whatever it is you have to say."

CHAPTER TEN

"WHEN I do, there might not be a wedding."

Alex clutched the rim of the pool. She had never fought so hard to remain in control. "From your demeanor I assumed as much." She swallowed hard. "Under normal circumstances engagements are made to be broken. That's what they're for, to see if both parties are ready for the big commitment. But there's nothing normal about your life, which has been in crisis for a very long time."

His rigid body seemed to tauten more, if that was possible.

"The ring I gave you didn't help. It reminded you of your duty and made everything all too real. Don't you know I understand?" she cried softly.

He breathed heavily. "That's the point. You don't." His voice was gruff.

She edged away from him a few inches. "Maybe not completely, but give me credit for realizing what this news will do to your father and mother. I'd do anything for you, Lucca, but I'm afraid in this case I don't know how to help you. This is a situation that needs the wisdom of Solomon to sort out."

"His wisdom would tell us a marriage based on a lie is no marriage."

Alex treaded water for a moment while she gathered her thoughts. "I agree, but I don't know what you're talking about. We were totally honest with each other. Regina knows everything. You said your parents are aware of the relationship with your lover, so what you just said doesn't make sense."

"Take my word for it, it does." His eyes closed tightly. "There's something I didn't tell you when I asked you to marry me."

"Lucca—if you're afraid to admit you have a child with this woman, don't be. The possibility did cross my mind. Is she afraid I'll keep you from recognizing it or some such crazy thing? I'd never do that to anyone. After growing up without my parents, I'd do everything in my power to help you make sure your son or daughter was welcomed and loved."

She heard a strange sound come from his throat before he smoothed his black hair off his forehead. "What if I told you there isn't another woman?"

Alex was pretty sure her face had gone a paste color, but she refused to fall apart now. "Do you mean you and Carlo? Sometimes I've felt he didn't like me, and I wondered if it was jealousy on his part."

"*Santa Vergine!* I'm almost afraid to hear what's going to come out of your mouth next. Obviously, that database in your mind has run through every possible conclusion except for the one answer not programmed. There were two reasons I lied to you.

"The first was because I owed my loyalty to Princess Sofia."

"Of San Marino?"

"So you know of her."

"Yes." Alex's love for Lucca had caused her to learn everything she could from Regina about the women in his life. She wasn't proud of her jealousy, which had driven her to look up their pictures on the Internet.

"We've been friends for many years and our parents wanted us to marry, but neither of us were inclined. Recently she confided that as soon as I got married she would forsake her title and live her life in Africa doing missionary work, but we've had to keep everything a secret for obvious reasons. Until she told me it was all right, I couldn't tell you."

Alexandra's chin lifted. "Instead you let me think she was a love interest. Why bother?"

She heard him draw in a labored breath as if this was the last thing he wanted to confess. "I didn't want you to think there was anything more to my proposal than a business transaction that would be beneficial to both of us."

Everything went dead inside Alex. "And that's what has caused all this needless suffering?" She laughed at him before getting out of the pool. Within seconds she'd slipped into her wrap and sandals.

"Don't you realize I know I'm the last woman any man would want unless he needs a consort within six hours? I thought you understood that, when we made our pact on the way to the airport. You didn't need to pretend Princess Sofia was your lover on my account.

"When I think of all the needless hours I've spent trying to figure out ways to help you…" Her eyes glittered like silver shards. "Well, now that you've gotten that off your chest, relax! Enjoy your swim! As for me, I'm going to bed and spend tomorrow with my family. If you're smart, you'll enjoy the bachelor party Regina told me your friends have planned for you."

She gave him the benefit of her full-bodied smile. "The next time we see each other will be in church. Hopefully we'll both stay upright throughout the ordeal. You're going to make a splendid king. *Ciao*, Lucca."

As soon as she reached her suite, she turned white-faced to her bodyguards trailing after her. "Would you two mind staying in here tonight as a special favor to me? One of you can lie on the lounger on the terrace, and the other on the couch in the sitting room. If anyone tries to come in either way, and I mean *anyone*, don't let them. Especially Lucca. It's bad luck for him to see me before the wedding."

She was thankful they'd be around till morning. Their presence would ensure she didn't sob her heart out all night. It would take her until the day after tomorrow to recover enough to get through the ceremony. Once she and Lucca went off on their honeymoon, he would learn the true meaning of a business transaction.

"You look so beautiful I can't believe it. That dress... The eggshell silk is perfect with your eyes, and the simplicity of it is pure genius on your figure."

Lucca's sister had come into her room at the last minute to walk downstairs with her. Alex had to admit the dress-maker had outdone herself. The cap sleeves and rounded neck were the right style for her.

"You're tall enough to wear something that flows and flows. At times like this I wish I could grow about four more inches."

"You're ravishing the way you are, Regina." Today she was in a filmy gown of the softest shade of lavender.

"I still don't understand why the dressmaker didn't fasten your diamond pin on it."

Alex could have told her why. Lucca had taken it back. No more pretense. "I'm not worried. I'm sure there's a perfectly logical explanation."

Regina frowned. "I hope so. My brother was in such a bad way this morning, everyone ran clear of him."

"It's called the bachelor blues. After his party he's feeling trapped."

"No, Alexandra. Something terrible was bothering him. He wouldn't talk to anybody."

"Well, he has to give a speech today. I don't suppose he's looking forward to it."

"He gives speeches all the time. That's not what's wrong. You really haven't seen him since night before last?"

"No. We went swimming and then we said good-night."

If Lucca had tried to come to her room in the last thirty-six hours, she didn't know about it. She'd purposely turned off the phones so there'd be no chance for communication. Her bodyguards had done everything for her. They were great.

"You look a vision, Alexandra!" Lucca's mother exclaimed. She swept into the room in a full-length gown of pale blue. In her arms she carried Alex's alençon lace veil. Behind her came the hairdresser holding a case.

"What's inside?"

His mother smiled. "Your own tiara. Lucca had it specially made for you to wear when you entertain and go to official functions."

He hadn't said anything about entertaining when he'd asked her to marry him.

"It's lightweight so your head won't ache. I think what he's had done with the diamond is stunning, don't you?"

The diamond?

Alex watched as the hairdresser lifted it from the velvet lining. The entire piece was so delicate and lacy it looked like a fairy crown strung with golden spider webs. There was only one jewel. The green teardrop dominated the center. Alex gasped, because the tiara was the perfect setting for it.

Once it was placed on her head, everyone helped drape the veil while the hairdresser secured it.

Lucca's mother kissed Alex's forehead. "You're a blessing to this family. We love you, my dear."

"I love you, too," Alex said with heartfelt emotion. Both of them wiped their tears away before Regina announced it was time.

"You're right." Her mother nodded. "My son went ahead half an hour ago. If I know him, and I do, he's waiting most impatiently for the first sight of his bride."

His very arranged bride.

The moment was bittersweet for so many reasons, not the least of them being the absence of both her parents. Yet no one could have been welcomed into a more wonderful family than the Vittorios.

Lucca's father would attend the ceremony, but arrangements had been made for him to leave if he felt too weak. This was such a huge day for father and son, Alex hoped Rudy would be able to see all of it.

It took an army of people to help Alex down the palace steps to the limo where her uncle was waiting. There was a stream of limos lined up on the north drive to take everyone to the fifteenth-century cathedral in the upper part of the city.

"What a glorious sight you make, Alexandra. I'm proud to be your great-uncle."

"Thank you, Uncle Yuri. You don't know what it means to me to have my family here."

"Lucca's a lucky man, but he already knows that."

Alex smiled but didn't respond.

"Are you all right?"

"Yes."

"Why do I get the feeling there's something wrong? You can tell me."

"I'm a little nervous."

"Today you're going to become Lucca's wife. His queen. You look like one. When we reach the cathedral, act like one. Lift your head high so that when everyone goes to bed tonight, they'll feel good knowing their new king is in the very best of hands."

Her uncle had a way of looking at life that was touching and oddly enough stiffened her backbone. She did have a role to play, albeit a much less important one. But she would do it and show Lucca she wasn't a person to be pitied. She leaned forward and caught his hand to squeeze it.

The city, lined with the royal flags, swarmed with people craning their necks to get a look as the limousine climbed the winding streets. It looked like the whole world had turned out for the coronation. After they stopped in front of the cathedral, everything became a blur.

Once Alex was helped out of the backseat, someone handed her a bouquet of white roses. Her uncle lowered the front of the veil over her face. Then he held her arm and they ascended the steps while dozens of photographers recorded their progress. She could hear organ music. People called to her and shouted, "Alexandra!"

Until they entered the cathedral, Alex smiled and turned her head to oblige them. Down the long aisle they walked, flanked by hundreds of beautifully dressed guests who filled the nave. The archbishop manned the pulpit. On his right stood Lucca, as straight as a lance and heartbreakingly resplendent in his white coronation suit and crown. He wore the wide blue ribbon from shoulder to waist that proclaimed him the crown prince.

Alex could see him through her veil, but she kept her eyes on his chest. He stepped forward to take her hand from Yuri and seat her next to him. Next to them sat his mother and father in full ceremonial dress. Her uncle sat down by Regina.

The whole time the archbishop led them in prayer, Lucca kept hold of her right hand in a firm grip while she balanced the roses with her left. When it ended, Lucca had perforce to let go of her and take his place in the centuries-old chair reserved for former sovereigns.

Wasting no time, the archbishop performed the rites. First the blue band was replaced with a red one, then Lucca's crown was exchanged for the larger crown that proclaimed him king. Following that process he gave his coronation speech in Italian. She only understood bits and pieces here and there. No matter how he'd hurt Alex, a feeling of such fierce pride and love for him swept over her she was afraid she couldn't contain it.

When his crown was removed, that was the signal for Regina to take the roses so Alex could stand by Lucca. At this point the archbishop led them in the wedding ceremony. Lucca did his part in Italian. Alex had been coached by Rudy's assistant so she knew when it came time to do her part in English. Despite Lucca's lack of affection for her, the vow she was about to make poured straight from her heart.

"I, Alexandra Carlisle Grigory, promise before the Church and Heaven to give my love, loyalty and devotion to my sovereign majesty and husband, His Royal Highness Lucca Umberto Schiaparelli Vittorio the Fifth, King of Castelmare, so help me God."

Lucca turned and lifted the veil with both hands. She kept her eyes level with his compelling mouth as he leaned closer. Inside the privacy of the lace hiding both their faces he whispered, "Why else would I have kidnapped you from the House of Savoy if I hadn't been totally and irrevocably in love with you?"

Alex came close to fainting from shock.

"But you wouldn't have believed love could happen that fast if I'd told you the truth. I used Sofia shamelessly to make you feel sorry for me because I wasn't about to return to Castelmare without you. I'd have said or done anything to have you, so be kind to me, *amore mio.*"

The kiss he gave her was a husband's kiss, hot with desire, bringing her to pulsating life so fast she started to weave and had to cling to the arms still holding up her veil. Outside the waves of ecstasy enveloping her body she heard the archbishop clear his throat.

"Lucca," she gasped quietly.

"You're my very heart. Tell me what I need to hear," he begged, "or I swear, my life means nothing."

"You *know* I love you. Now please—"

"Your word is my command, *bellissima.*"

He arranged the veil behind the tiara. She knew her face was scarlet, but as Lucca took hold of her hand, she remembered her uncle's advice and held her head high. The organ began to play and everyone got to their feet.

Lucca's thumb made provocative circles against her palm as they walked down the aisle. The moment they stepped outside the doors, she heard the cheers of the crowd.

"Viva il re! Viva Alexandra!"

The sound of church bells pealed sonorously over the city. But even louder were the fireworks shooting off inside her body as he kissed her again to the delight of their onlookers.

Together they descended the steps to the horse-drawn coach waiting at the bottom. As Lucca helped her inside, their eyes met. "We managed to stay upright, but don't plan on being in that position any longer than it takes for us to reach the yacht."

Alex wondered if her cheeks would ever go back to their normal color. "Have you no shame, Your Majesty?"

His white smile dazzled her. "None at all, Your Majesty." He climbed in next to her. A footman closed the door. "As breathtaking as you look," he murmured against her mouth, "there's one sight I haven't seen yet. I've been living for it.

"Now wave to the crowd. They came to look at you. Today you're making history, *mia moglie.*"

His wife. The most beautiful word in the world.

"Darling? Don't you think we should get up, if only to let your crew know we're alive?"

Lucca pulled her higher across his chest, trapping her with his powerful legs. "Every time the steward takes back another empty tray to the kitchen, he knows there are two people creating their own paradise."

She covered his impossibly handsome face with kisses, unable to get enough of him. "But it's been three days."

"Is my wife embarrassed because we haven't left the bedchamber in all that time?"

"No." She slid her arms around his neck. Looking into his slumberous black eyes she said, "I don't care if the whole world knows we've been this happy. Do you suppose Carlo has told your father?"

The smile she loved broke out on his face. "You mean, that we've been working on his grandchild day and night? There's no doubt about it. Did I tell you I've been having the time of my life in the process? Come closer, you gorgeous thing."

Alex needed no urging. Their mouths fused in passion. Once more the joy of making love with her husband surpassed all other experiences. There was no end to his giving or hers. At times the beauty of it brought her to tears.

"I don't ever want to do anything else," she admitted an hour later, temporarily sated by rapture. He looked down at her and his hands stilled in her hair. A look of profound seriousness had entered his eyes. "What is it?" she asked, so attuned to him already it was as if they were one.

"I never wanted to be king, but I've changed my mind."

Her breath caught. "Why is that?"

"These past three days have shown me a whole new life. I've discovered I want to spend as much of it as possible with you. We'll do everything together. Unlike most men who don't take their wives to work, it's expected that I involve you in the country's affairs.

"What's wonderful about the palace is that my home and my work place are under the same roof. We'll always be together, always travel together."

Alex couldn't believe what she was hearing. "My secret dream growing up was to find one man who would love only me and want to be with me all the time, but I didn't think it was possible."

"It's more than possible," he said before plundering her mouth once more. Time passed before she became cognizant of it again. They ended up lying on their sides holding each other.

"I want to make up for all your years of loneliness."

She cupped his handsome face in her hands. "You already have. I'm so happy it hurts, Lucca."

"Then you have some idea of how I feel. To think I found you on the very day I'd given up hope of ever knowing true fulfillment."

Alex ran a hand through his hair. "No one but a person like the Princess Sofia knows the kind of burden you've had to bear. Do you think Regina feels it the same way?"

"Yes," he whispered against her lips. "Papa ingrained it into her that she's second in line to the throne. No matter what, she'll always do her duty."

"Just like you. But what if she never meets a royal she loves the way we love each other?"

Lucca sighed into her neck. "I lie awake nights worrying about that. I'd give anything for my sister to know the kind of ecstasy you and I have found, but I refuse to worry about it right now. This time is for us, *squisita.*"

"Oh, darling." She half sobbed with joy, unable to stop covering his face with kisses. *"Ti amo,"* she said against his eyes. *"Sono innamorata di te,"* she whispered against his jaw. *"Ti adoro,"* she mouthed the words against his lips.

"Someone's been teaching you besides me," he growled into her neck.

"I asked Professor Emilio to help me with some phrases for the honeymoon."

Lucca let go with full-bodied laughter. The happy sound reached right down inside her soul.

"Did I say them right?" Her beautiful gray eyes beseeched him.

He sobered. "*Perfetto*. I'm the luckiest man alive, Alexandra. We were meant to be together."

"I wanted to belong to you the moment you commanded me in your monarch voice, 'Come back and sit down, Signorina Grigory. I'm not through with you.'"

Lucca crushed her in his arms. "I was a monster. I don't know how you put up with me. Love me again so I know I'm not dreaming," he whispered urgently. "I've only begun to live."

REQUEST YOUR FREE BOOKS!
2 FREE NOVELS PLUS 2
FREE GIFTS!

From the Heart, For the Heart

HR08R

You're invited to join our Tell Harlequin Reader Panel!

By joining our new reader panel you will:

- Receive Harlequin® books—they are FREE and yours to keep with no obligation to purchase anything!
- Participate in fun online surveys
- Exchange opinions and ideas with women just like you
- Have a say in our new book ideas and help us publish the best in women's fiction

In addition, you will have a chance to win great prizes and receive special gifts! See Web site for details. Some conditions apply. Space is limited.

To join, visit us at

www.TellHarlequin.com.

Coming Next Month

Available March 10, 2009

**Spring is here and romance is in the air this month
as Harlequin Romance® takes you on a whirlwind journey
to meet gorgeous grooms!**

#4081 BRADY: THE REBEL RANCHER Patricia Thayer

Second in the **Texas Brotherhood** duet. Injured pilot Brady falls for the
lovely Lindsey Stafford, but she has secrets that could destroy him. Now
Brady must fight again, this time for love....

#4082 ITALIAN GROOM, PRINCESS BRIDE Rebecca Winters

We visit the **Royal House of Savoy** as Princess Regina's arranged
wedding day approaches. Royal gardener Dizo has one chance to risk
all—and claim his princess bride!

#4083 FALLING FOR HER CONVENIENT HUSBAND Jessica Steele

Successful lawyer Phelix isn't the same shy teenager Nathan
conveniently wed eight years ago. He hasn't seen her since, and her
transformation hasn't escaped the English tycoon's notice....

#4084 CINDERELLA'S WEDDING WISH Jessica Hart

In Her Shoes...
Celebrity playboy Rafe is *not* Miranda's idea of Prince Charming. But
when she's hired as his assistant, Miranda is shocked to learn that Rafe
has hidden depths.

#4085 HER CATTLEMAN BOSS Barbara Hannay

When Kate inherits half a run-down cattle station, she doesn't expect to
have a sexy cattleman boss, Noah, to contend with! As they toil under
the hot sun, romance is on the horizon....

#4086 THE ARISTOCRAT AND THE SINGLE MOM Michelle Douglas

Handsome English aristocrat Simon keeps to himself. But, thrown into
the middle of single mom Kate's lively family on a trip to Australia, Simon
finds his buttoned-up manner slowly undone.

HRCNMBPA0209